# It Is Written

# It Is Written

Kelvin L. Singleton

ISBN Paperback: 978-0-9979041-3-0

Printed in the United States of America

Interior Design: Ghislain Viau

*I dedicate this venture to my mother, Marcella Singleton.*
*May God bless and keep her soul. It is also dedicated to my daughter,*
*Keturha K. Singleton, the greatest thing to ever come from me.*

# Contents

CHAPTER I

# Where Life Imitates Death

It is a hot Southern night. No breeze circulates the stagnant air near the ground, but an occasional cloud passes before the face of the full moon on high. When lunar glory returns to the night sky over Conway, South Carolina, the weeping willows along the winding path became luminous, brooding hulks. The lone whippoorwill's ominous lament echoes throughout the surrounding darkness, as if it hears the summons of death, then falls silent when someone approaches.

Drenched with sweat, the old preacher limps up the hill. Reverend Drover's heaving lungs drag oxygen from the air and expel steam as he stops to catch his breath. He leans on the shotgun to rub his bleeding left leg in an area where the sticky burs cling to his pants. The cotton rag tied above his knee is soaked with blood. His red eyes are downcast, burdened by burning tears that flow down his cheeks while he offers God a silent prayer of forgiveness. He knows that he should turn back, go home to tend his dead. However, when he hears the old Ford truck whining up the dirt road above, he sees their sightless eyes and bloodstained faces.

The preacher's eyes shut against the crimson image that streaked the floor as he dragged the bodies toward the door of the smoke-filled home. He'd found his wife impaled by a rusty pitchfork on the back porch. His only son had been bludgeoned and cleaved. His daughters, both virgins, had been brutally raped and defiled before dying.

Because the newly dead are not easily silenced, the preacher jams his clenched fists to his ears in a futile attempt to thwart their horrid screams. The utter brutality of it all suddenly comes crashing down upon him, driven deeper into his reality with every throbbing pulse.

The ugliness of what he failed to prevent causes slivers of ice to form just beneath the skin, moving like paper-thin, razoredged glaciers that seem bent on separating the man from his flesh. The weight of a soul-deep shiver causes his cracked lips to wail into the echoing night.

Reverend Drover forces his bleeding leg to carry him up the hill, using the shotgun to support his hurried steps. He arrived too late to save his family, but their killers are approaching, and he has to be there to greet them at the top of the hill.

His eyes are wildly ablaze. Standing with his aching legs apart, he shuffles a shell into the shotgun's chamber and utters, "Yes, Lord. I am become wrath and vengeance." His thoughts are like ripples on still water, barely a whisper by the time the words part his bleeding lips.

Though dressed in black when the headlights hit him, the preacher's eyes and collar are clearly illuminated. The startled driver turns the wheel harshly to the right, and the shotgun roars as two men are ejected from the bed of the truck. Lead pellets shred their bodies in midair like giant quail in flight. Both are dead when they hit the ground, tumbling to a halt where their blood will soak the earth.

The old preacher fires through a cloud of dust as the driver fights for control of the bouncing vehicle. The last man in the rear of the truck holds onto the wooden rails for dear life.

He is tossed into the air as his right arm slips between the slats. The bones snap like dried twigs, but the arm does not come free when he is thrown over the top of the railing. He screams while dangling from his unnaturally bent limb, caught as the heels of his boots batter the cab of the lurching vehicle.

As the truck barrels toward the church, the preacher's fourth volley ravages his right leg and abdomen and claim the driver's life as well. When the tires hit a flowerbed, the front end plows through the graying wall of the Mount Zion Baptist Church. Splintered wood, two oil lamps, and Bibles are scattered among the pews inside. The very torch they brought to burn the church to the ground is flung within, to do its work despite the man of God's interception.

The preacher ignores the moans and groans of the trapped man with the broken arm. He hears the passenger door creaking open as the last man falls to the wooden floor inside. Their leader, that evil, vile, bastard of a man, is the last of them.

As the bruised and battered passenger crawls toward the altar, the preacher kicks the doors in and proceeds inside. When the murderer backs himself against the altar, the preacher limps within a yard to ram the gun barrel through his front teeth.

Reverend Drover does not pull the trigger because he found only four shells for the shotgun before bolting up the path to catch them. He withdraws the barrel and casts the weapon aside as the wounded man pleads for his life.

The preacher now bellows broken scriptures as he pulls a long machete from his belt. With the blade raised high, he declares, "Barnes, vengeance is mine, says the Lord. But on this night, Demon, I am owed an eye for an eye and a life for a life!"

Reverend Drover yanks the white collar from his neck, and

the blade slices through the air! It comes down repeatedly, slinging blood and bile until its work is done. Holy fire blazes well into the night. The billowing black smoke, mixed with the agonized screams of the preacher, is Mount Zion's final cry to heaven.

Fifty-one years later, the bloodshot eyes of Judge Barnes open to search the sweat-soaked darkness, but he is alone. No one knows that he witnessed the killings all those years ago, because none were left alive to see him crawl from under the tarp just as it had caught fire. No one noticed the tracks of the ten-year-old in the dirt, leading a slight blood trail away from Mount Zion. No one saw him, other than God.

CHAPTER 2

*Braided Leather*

By the year 1999, the glory days of the Ku Klux Klan seem like shrieking ghosts in the wind. Those rabid times are long gone, but past sins often seek resurrection from the grave. There are too many similarities to be coincidental; things that should never have been written down. If this novel is any indication, someone knows of things that they should not.

From the lips of a self-righteous man spew the words, "When judgment comes, he'll not smile upon you. He will not pray for your wretched soul. When judgment comes, he will show you no mercy, for his just punishment must fit your crimes. When swift vengeance comes for you, his barren embrace will sear you to the quick and freeze you to the core. Even then, though there can be no redemption, there shall be but a momentary quiet for the soul of the damned. This has been so decreed by the very mouth of God Almighty!"

SHWIPTTT! Lash number twenty-nine cracks the silence in the early morning stillness. Three feet of braided leather sings out as it wraps around the dark brown flesh. Its forked tongue is deftly withdrawn just before touching itself in the center of the young man's exposed back. Again, it lays him open to the bone, parting his flesh like tall grass in a furious wind.

Again, with what could be his last breath, he whimpers, "I didn't do it. God help me. I didn't kill that old lady!"

SHWIPTTT! The thirtieth lash cries out. Although the leathery tool of punishment snakes out at twelve feet, it is only the last thirty-six inches that sings. The soaked end serenades where its forked leather tongues transform into deadly razors made for pain and built for cutting flesh.

Initially it has been a quiet night, a relative void that is broken only by the slow tapping of the officer's heels on the cool concrete floor. The holding cells of the county lockup are unusually empty on this Saturday night.

To the left, a drunk twitches in his sleep. His mumbling is due to a fitful dream of an angry wife who swears that he is on his own this time.

A bandaged and bruised barfly, who had the misfortune of meeting the mumbling man, sleeps in the opposite cell. As he snoozes, whistling overtones emanate from his swollen nostrils. He also dreams of recent hours, when he met a fellow drinker at the Night Horse. They shared a few drinks, griping about life, women, and politics. An argument about the bar tab led to broken chairs and spilled liquor.

The tapping heels turn the corner, halting abruptly. The wired window at the far end has been disturbed. To the officer's dismay, the last two cells are empty.

The alarm shatters the quiet, raising the dead at 3:45 a.m. Fifteen minutes later, Judge Barnes listens to the television as he cinches his tie and pops in his dentures. The phone rings as he pauses before the television screen where a story of great interest now breaks.

"The suspects in the robbery/murder of Alice Lukasavage, the night clerk at the Quick Stop gas station at the corner of Rawlins and Anthem, have escaped from the Conway County lockup, where they were being held for Monday morning arraignment. It is possible that a temporary, yet unexplained, power outage catalyzed the escape. The nineteen-year-old suspect, Edward Travis, and twenty-two-year-old Thomas Glass, were arrested on Saturday afternoon by the Conway County Sheriff Department. The two African-American men were taken to the county lockup, from which they escaped mere hours later. Officials say that the cell doors must have unlocked during the power outage. The suspects then managed to escape through a wired window. Officials say that they have no idea how Edward Travis and Thomas Glass could have broken out without tools or making enough noise to alert duty officers. Concerned citizens feel that the alleged suspects may have received help, but such rumors are unfounded at this time."

Her teleprompter flickers, causing a slight hesitation from the reporter. "Police are warning that the escapees may be armed and should be considered extremely dangerous. The members of the State Law Enforcement Department and local law enforcement agencies investigating the escape are currently involved in a tri-county manhunt. The alleged suspect, Edward Travis, was arrested Saturday afternoon during a routine traffic stop. Reportedly, Officer Nicholas Sherman thought he detected the smell of marijuana. During the search for drugs, police found the credit card of the slain convenience-store worker and mother of three. Sources allege that it was the fingerprint evidence found on the credit card that later linked Travis's friend, Thomas Glass, to the murder. However, the Chief of Police and District Attorney McBride have denied making what they both consider to be an inappropriate statement."

With dawn upon the hillside, Thomas Erin Glass flinches, certain that he is next to feel the sting that strips flesh from bone. His entire being is caught in the confines of some static-charged current that vibrates throughout his core. Every lash of the whip brings a cry of agony from the busted lips of his best friend, Edward Travis.

Crack! The forked leather slashes into Edward's back as he swings suspended. One more lash among thirty-one opens a new wound as the murder suspect screams for mercy. Throughout the blood and butchery, Thomas Glass watches every stroke.

Blood drips from Travis's toes to pool below his feet, seeping slowly between the cracks in the planked floor of the old barn.

Now drained of fight and denial, Edward Travis finally abandons the most important truth of his life and death. Though it avails nothing, he confesses to a murder that he did not commit. The saturated rope creaks as Edward Travis swings lazily with his chin upon his ravaged chest. The young man dies with his eyes open. His broken, swollen lips will cry out no more. His back, chest, and arms have been laid open by thirty-nine savage lashes. Nevertheless, his painful suffering is forever over and amen.

While kneeling in a pool of urine and tears, Thomas Glass observes as the glistening knife slices through the rope to send Edward Travis's emaciated body crashing to the floor before him. He is startled when a heavy engine growls to life in the distance. The sound of the diesel can only mean that they are digging a hole.

Moments later, just as Christ was forced to carry the cross, Thomas Glass must drag his dead friend to their grave. To his left and right, before and aft, the condemned man struggles amidst thirteen jurors. Glass has spent most of these torturous hours stripped to his dingy, soiled underwear and shackled about the ankles. The very rope that held Edward Travis aloft while the whip sung its deadly hymn now binds his wrists.

Acidic sweat stings Glass's wounds, which are minor compared to those of his friend. His eyes bulge as his heart hammers a spasmodic rhythm of doom in his ears. The young man cries and whimpers for mercy, knowing that his own death will be a thing of brutal beauty and pain.

These wordless, masked men are escorting Thomas Glass at a pace that suggests ritual; that they have done this before. There is no hurry, and each passing moment becomes a theme of torture.

Glass staggers across fallen branches and unforgiving pinecones that bite at his bare feet. When he looks down at the dead eyes of his best friend, they are portals of agony, visual records of Edward's final moment. Twigs litter his kinky, black hair. His ravaged skin is a montage of clinging leaves and pine needles as he is dragged forth.

Glass stumbles, trying to free himself of the bloody rope. Repeatedly he screams, "I'm sorry. I'm so sorry, Eddie. I didn't mean for this to happen!"

From where he kneels upon the ground, members of the halted procession seem as tall as the surrounding trees. When the blue, blue sky starts to reel, the almighty whip cracks the air to force him back to reality.

The grave is deep when the backhoe's job is complete. When its rumbling engine rattles to a stop, there is a moment of utter silence. No birds are chirping near this morbid clearing. No squirrels are chattering from their nests on high, but they are watching.

Glass is facing the broad side of a huge truck. By looking beneath it, he can see the pit on the other side. From its bed, a length of chain runs to the base of a sturdy tree.

The silence is again broken when the truck's engine belches to life. When it lurches forward, there comes a grating protest. The murderer watches as the chain draws tight, dragging a concrete slab from the bed. It slams upon the ground before the pit, shaking the earth to raise a cloud of dust with a resounding boom!

The driver repositions the truck on the far side, about ten yards beyond that gruesome gouge in the earth. That abhorrent thing it has deposited on the ground is most certainly an instrument of death. The pillar is two feet thick and eight feet in length, three feet wide and weighing at least two tons. Mass, however, is not its most forbidding aspect. This thing is riddled with jagged iron bars that protrude toward the doomed prisoner like rusting teeth.

The driver of the four-wheeler leaves the engine running while he drags a long, steel chain from the bed toward the grave. With one end secured to the trailer hitch, someone leaps upon the concrete slab to catch the chain. He kneels to tie the end of the chain to a nylon rope that runs through a circle in the center of the pillar. Now he pulls the short rope to draw the chain through.

Like the darkest of shadows, understanding finally falls upon the brow of Thomas Glass.

He is seized and held still while the chain is hauled toward him. His screams for mercy are unheeded as the chain is secured to the thick leather harness about his waistline.

As Glass thrashes about the ground, pulling at his restraints like a trapped animal, the man who presides over his trial and execution stands between him and the pillar. He is holding the Bible in one hand and a novel in the other, staring at a coward who confessed to murdering the convenience store clerk only after watching his innocent friend's enduring torture.

From the novel found on the front seat of Edward Travis's car, Judge Barnes paraphrases, "When judgment comes, I'll not smile upon you. I will not pray with you, nor weep for your wretched soul. When judgment comes, I will show you no mercy—for this just punishment must fit your crimes."

Ignored as he begs for his life, Glass struggles to his knees. His onlookers show no emotion. There is no laughter and no expression of joy in his moment of terror. They are silently staring down upon him, unmoved.

Glass's memory of the murder flashes before his eyes. What he stole in cash did not supply him with enough drugs to satisfy his craving through the night. Nevertheless, he knows upon the precipice of doom that no amount would have been worth the life taken, let alone three. Now spurned by man, he prays to God for the first time in years.

The engine revs, belching black smoke into the still morning air. Again, it revs and the wheels began to spin, churning dirt and dead leaves into a cloud. As the truck speeds away, the chain sings its own song while drawn through the hole in the concrete pillar.

Thomas Glass grunts when snatched forward, screaming with his legs flailing about like a rag doll in a cloud of dust. He continues to shriek as he rushes to meet the iron bars of the mangler.

Suddenly the front end of the truck bows when the brakes lock up. Glass opens his eyes one at a time, breathing hard like a fledgling whose mother has been gone too long. He whimpers a sigh of short-lived relief, lying on his right side because the harness has shifted. His skin burns, tingling all over as the dust begins to settle.

His voice cracks when he cries, "Thank you, Jesus. Thank you!" However, when the truck revs again, he feels a menacing presence behind him. His breath freezes when he rolls slightly to the left. Merely inches away, those gnarled and rusted tentacles stand at pause.

The engine revs and the truck rocks forward, causing him to panic. He tries pulling away by using the rope that drags his dead friend for the joyless ride, but Edward is laying face down a few feet away. His outstretched arms have been drawn extremely taut by the rope that cinches those swollen, meshed fingers into a single immortal fist. His mouth came open while being dragged, and the lower jaw has dug a trench in the ground to fill it with sod. The body barely moves when Glass yanks on the rope because roots now anchor his lower front teeth.

This is it, that momentary silence for the soul of the damned. However, because there can be no redemption, the truck eases forward. Ever so slowly, Edward's lower jaw opens until the skin of his cheeks split at the corner of his lips. The bone hinges of his lower jaw shatter just before the teeth are torn from the gum.

Glass gurgles as the longest iron bar pierces his skin. The liver and spleen are punctured just as multiple points of contact begin to gush. At the back of his skull, three jagged points threaten. No matter how he moves, at least two of them are unavoidable. He shrieks in agony when the truck revs and lurches forward to ram a bloody spear through his left eye.

The driver hits the gas and lets go of the clutch. When Glass slams into the pillar, a crimson mist explodes from his punctured skin. The chain snaps at its weakest link, but not before its bloody job is done. The pillar moves, crying out as it upends into the waiting pit with streaks of red marring its grayish skin.

The judge looks down at the novel and says, "We've got to cut off the head of this black viper. Only then will this unholy body die."

He thinks better of tossing the novel into the grave. This bitter pill could only have been conceived by the wicked imagination of someone who has dug too deeply into the past. What he has already read of it strikes too closely to home. Because this novel is the resurrection of dark and malignant acts, fiendishly disguised as fiction, it needs testing to the very end.

CHAPTER 3

## *The Fan*

*T*he alluring woman reads, "'It is written within the crimson annals of humanity that with every tragic death, whether due to racial intolerance or the scourge of war, the inhabitants of this world are irrevocably diminished. We have fallen short the aspirations of whatever deities we acknowledge by defeating our canon upon this world with petulant self-pursuits. Our species murders its own brilliance by accentuating minor differences, giving way to those who prey upon impressionable minds to widen the breach in a narrow-minded belief in one chosen people. It is our very diversity that contains the key to our evolutionary pinnacle, for each culture and race contributes something vital to the growth and beauty of this world. If we do not bind the devils of separatism, we may never achieve that which God has aspired in our very creation. With great diligence we must defuse and dismantle their many weapons of division, lest someday our children may take up those arms to become killers themselves.'"

Damara Byrd sighs, wiping a tear from her eye before returning her gaze. "When I first read that paragraph, I cried, Mr. Prophet. I cried because it's so true."

The author smiles. "Then my work is done. That may seem a rather macabre thing to say, but it's how I always feel when someone says something like that to me," he maintains. "I suppose it gives me a sense of accomplishment. Not in the fact that something I've written has caused someone to cry, but in that I've touched in them something deep down inside. Thank you."

"Believe me, you've touched many. When I read *Diminished*, it reminded me of all the reasons I left Texas. When my cousin was dragged to death, I knew I had to go. I was very concerned about leaving my family to go so far away, especially my mother and little brother. But you know, leaving Jasper and moving to Manhattan is the best thing that ever happened to me," the fashion model says.

"Are you related to James Byrd, the murder victim?" the writer asks with macabre curiosity.

"Yes. He may not have been a perfect angel, but he didn't deserve to die that way. No one does. Murder, hatred and racial intolerance really do diminish us by leaps and bounds," Damara says thoughtfully.

"Well said, Ms. Byrd." The writer sighs. "It would be nice to go to my grave knowing that something I've written has made a positive impact on people."

"No doubt. I still can't believe that I'm actually sharing a first-class flight with Killian Prophet—the Black Assassin himself. My girlfriends are going to fall out!"

"You're too much," he says.

"Will you autograph this copy for me? I hate to impose."

"Not a problem." With pen in hand, he autographs her copy of his fifth novel.

"It must have been fate that my friend decided to return this book just before I left New York. However, *Black Tide Rising* intrigued the hell out of me. I found myself sitting up at three in the morning with all the lights on, and I was chewing off all my fingernails. Now, I'm a black woman, so I can imagine the effect it had on some of the white people that read it. God!"

He is flattered by her words of praise. "Have you read all of my books?"

She smiles. "I liked them all, but that was my favorite. I started to hear those ominous voodoo drums in my sleep. I'm sorry, but I don't think you'll ever top it."

"I must admit—I'm very proud of that one."

"You should be. If you don't mind my asking, just what prompted you to write that story? Did the idea just pop into your mind one day?" He hands her the book. "Thanks."

"Well, that's a story in itself," he says in reflection. "I believe it was stewing in the back of my mind since college. I was in my dorm room when some crazy white boys from the floor came to me and insisted that I listen to something. I went back to their room, where they dialed a 900 number. Naturally, I thought they were calling a sleazy sex line, but it was far from that."

Enthralled by the story, she turns in her seat to ask, "What did you hear?"

"It was an election year, and the line belonged to an independent presidential candidate. I can't recall his name, but he was campaigning under the flag of something called the

Southern White Patriot's Party."

"The Southern what?"

"Oh yeah. This person actually thought that the poison spewing from his lips was going to get him elected. Among other things, he described African-Americans as slant-eyed, bubble lipped, kinky-haired, mud-colored mongrels."

"Oh my goodness!"

"The man had it honest. I don't know what he had for certain, but he had it honest. Anyway, the candidate said something that stayed in the back of my mind until I finally wrote that story. He was putting down Caucasian males for wanting to come home after a hard day at work, just to sit down with a six pack and watch the niggers play basketball on TV."

Despite her mild amusement, Damara grunts with disgust.

"Now this is the part that got to me. He quoted some statistical figures that I later checked out and found to be true. He said that while they were watching basketball, black people were having babies four to one compared to whites. I began to wonder. Just think of it. If that were true, just how long would it take us to catch up and surpass the white populous? That's where I got the idea for *Black Tide Rising*. It's ironic that I may owe my most successful novel to the ravings of a straight-up racist." They giggle at the thought.

"I'll say. He'd probably kill himself if he found out. When I read it, I actually started to wonder if it could be fact. Many people did," she says. "I mean, when you really think about it, the story may not be so farfetched. How in the world did you get it published?"

"It wasn't easy, that's for sure. I'd begun to consider investing my own money when my agent called with the good news. We needed someone, no matter what his racial orientations and religious beliefs, who could look to the book's marketability. She was finally able to find the raw capitalist that we needed to produce such a controversial story," he says.

Killian Prophet finds this conversation refreshing. Ms. Byrd differs from many of his fans because she is unobtrusive, attentive, and a very polite young woman.

"Calling it controversial is an understatement, Mr. Prophet. You turned the mother out," she says with a gleam in her eyes. "Some of our more fanatical brothers and sisters were talking civil war. Even my mother took it to heart—after she got over the religious implications in the beginning, of course. Two days after she stopped calling you a devil-worshipping heathen, my mother was ready to grab her butcher's knife and go to slicin' and dicin'." Her original accent, her Texas accent, is beginning to resurface.

Killian bursts into laughter and catches himself before disturbing any sleeping passengers. She too glances about the airplane guiltily.

"So I'm a devil-worshipping heathen? I now know for sure that I've been called everything but a child of God. However, it is unfortunate that too many people, including some of our own, judge me by my book covers. I'm often accused of being a racist with a separatist agenda, but they don't get that it's exactly the opposite that I hope to achieve. I'm forced to conclude that many of those who can't get past the title or first couple of pages seem to think I'm talking about them—especially when it's about drugs or hate crimes. You wouldn't believe some of the whack jobs out there."

"You wanna bet?" she chuckles. "I'm a fashion model, living in New York. You seem to be in good shape. Come to the set and strut your tighty-whities down the runway for me and I'll show you whack jobs, Mr. Prophet."

Killian blushes as the seatbelt announcement is made. Wilmington, North Carolina, is beneath them, finally.

Though he is anxious to be on his way, he hates landing just as much as taking off. As the airliner begins its descent, he closes his eyes and inhales Damara Byrd's perfume, which is one of the fragrances preferred by his wife. He smiles to himself, knowing that he will see Miranda and Tressa soon. With only a short drive to Wilmington Beach, he will be home again.

Forty-five minutes after Flight 301 lands, Killian Prophet pulls into the garage. He has grown accustomed to seeing his wife standing in the door to the kitchen when he returns. There is but a minor twinge of disappointment as the garage door closes behind him.

He drops his luggage on the floor, looking at the vacant couch in the living room where his wife is sure to have fallen asleep. She is not there.

As Killian turns the corner on his way to the stairs, he comes face to face with Miranda, who's dressed in a white teddy and draped in a short silk top that shows off her legs. She is leaning on the wall with her arms crossed, smiling at her startled husband, just leaning there with her head tilted to the wall. The flames of the fireplace are hypnotic reflections within the depths of her dreamy, brown eyes.

Her smile causes his knees to wilt. Powerless, he assumes the same position, just her opposite. They gaze into each other's eyes, feeling the moment.

She reaches for his middle button, holding it fast. "How I've missed you, Husband. Your tall, bronzed image has invaded mine every waking thought. Night after endless night, these longing arms have reached for you, only to find your cold, empty pillow where I was forced to seek my comforts." Miranda Prophet draws him near.

"Touch me, kind Sir, and you will set my soul afire. With but a simple kiss, I will swoon beneath those burning lips, for it is within your arms that I am truly alive."

With little time and space between them, their lips meet. The kiss is long and tender, ending with them giggling like school kids.

Killian caresses her back and shoulders. "I don't know, Miranda. Marrying a playwright may not have been such a good idea."

She hikes her shoulders playfully. "Do you see the sort of honeydew drivel I tend to write when you're not here? You're only good for my career when you're around, Mr. Prophet."

"Hmm. I kind of liked it, actually. I especially liked the part where you talked about your loins being warm for me."

"I didn't say that. Did I say that?" she teases.

"Oh, I'm sorry. My own loins must have been getting warm for you."

She coos and draws her hips closer to his. They kiss, moaning in unison as if rehearsed. When their lips part, she says, "Hmm. Maybe I did say it. Come to think of it, I believe I did."

"You know you're crazy, right?" he asks. "Kiss me, you fool."

She backs away. "As much as I'd like to oblige our carnal desires, I wouldn't feel right about keeping you all to myself while your number-one fan is waiting."

"Daddy, you're back!"

"See what I mean?" Miranda says.

Tressa is running down the stairs. When her father reaches the bottom step, she launches herself into his arms with the pure trust of a child.

Killian catches his six-year-old daughter and spins around. When he stops, Tressa rains kisses on his cheeks.

Miranda marvels at the connection between Killian and Tressa as they airplane up the steps. At the top, he spins until she screams with joy. "I'm dizzy, Daddy!"

"Me, too. Whatever will we do?" he asks while stumbling a bit for added effect.

Miranda leads him down the hall. "I've got you two drunks."

Moments later, after catching his breath, Killian kisses Tressa's cheeks. She is unusually anxious to go to sleep because a special day is fast approaching.

When Killian leaves his daughter's room, a gust of wind tells him where to find his wife.

Miranda is standing before the balcony door, where the sheer white curtains and her long, jet-black hair flutters with the cooling breeze. Her nipples have frosted in the chilly night air, calling him unto them. No words are uttered as they sway throughout the moment, sharing a visual link that speaks of undying love.

Fifty yards away, while the choppy water laps against the boat's hull, a stranger with the binoculars grunts. With the soggy stump of the cigar tucked in the right corner of his lips, he spits. The watcher mutters to himself, "Now that's true love. Must be nice."

This stranger watches them for a while, even as their intimacy grows. When the bedroom lights go dim, he puts away the tools of his trade and zips the insulated camouflage coat to his neckline. He slips on a pair of goggles and pulls the hood up to protect his head from the wind.

Looking back at the house once more, he turns the key to start the outboard motor. Throttling her gently, he maneuvers the boat farther into obscurity. Soon he is gone, unseen and unnoticed.

# CHAPTER 4

# *Dancer*

*I*n slow motion, Tressa flies through the air with her arms stretched wide. When she crash-lands between her sleeping parents, raising them from the depths of slumber, she plants kisses on their cheeks with equal enthusiasm.

Killian yawns wide. "Somebody's up very early today. I wonder why that is."

Miranda yawns into a fist. Both parents are flexing their eyelids.

"Good morning, Mommy. I love you."

"Good morning, Sweetheart. I love you, too," Miranda says while looking into Tressa's gleeful eyes. "Do you know what day this is, Tressa?"

"It's a very special day, Little One," Killian whispers.

Tressa kneels between them, tossing her hands into the air and shouting, "It's happy birthday to me. Yeah!" She claps her hands overhead.

Her parents raise their hands in the air and shout, "Yeah!"

"I'm hungry, Daddy. Can we have the blue pancakes? What do you think, Mommy?"

"That sounds pretty good to me. Do you think we can convince your old man to make them for us?"

Tressa looks at her father with a most disarming smile and says, "I love you, Daddy."

"Oh, now you love me, too. I see." He looks at his wife and says, "It would be my pleasure to make breakfast for my favorite girls."

Tressa claps her hands. Her father is about to get out of bed when he remembers that he's naked. Miranda laughs at his embarrassment and sends Tressa to brush her teeth.

When the child leaves, Miranda says, "Lord knows that child must really love us."

As Killian puts on his pajama bottom, he grunts. "Why do you say it like that?"

Miranda chuckles for a second. "How else could she stand our morning breath? Yuck!"

"The child is a saint." He rejoins Miranda on the bed, but when the dragon rears its ugly head, there is a race for the mouthwash. After breakfast, father and daughter will go on a special outing.

There is a slight chill in the shade today. Most of the big cats are lounging about with very little interest in the sparse zoo visitors. Seska, the big Bengal female, is pacing back and forth along the western wall. She seems quite pensive, looking upward as if expecting something.

Tressa asks, "Daddy, why do they have to be locked up? Why can't they be free like us?"

Killian smiles because, above all others, they share a special affinity for the striped cats. He might have asked a similar question as a child himself.

He clears his throat. "Well, Tressa, that's a good question. They have to stay inside of this habitat for their own good. You see, I think that tigers are colorblind. They can't really tell the difference in colors at traffic lights. They don't understand that green means that you can go, or that red means to stop, so they can get hurt by cars."

"Okay. I understand. When they learn their colors, they can go free," she says.

"You got it."

Tressa leans on the railing and points at the left sleeve of her jacket. "Seska," she says, "this is blue. Remember that."

It's almost time for the birthday party. Killian Prophet hugs his daughter, thanking God for her while wishing that she could stay innocent forever.

Back at home, Tressa is busy from the moment everyone yells, "Surprise!" Several video cameras will capture the events of her seventh birthday party. Many of Tressa's schoolmates have come to share this moment.

The magician amazes the kids with her illusions. The clowns dazzle them with their silly antics. The sound of joyful children abounds at the Wilmington Beach home. Balloons have bloomed like flowers throughout the house and backyard, filling Tressa's world with the colors of happiness. The hot dogs and hamburgers are good, but the punch, ice cream, and cake will flow like manna in a child's perfect version of heaven.

Each recorded and unrecorded moment grows more special for the child and her proud parents. The games and gifts are merely facets of a special occasion that rings with joy.

Killian's parents, Anders and Ethyl Prophet, came up from Charleston for the day. They will leave before dark because they are going on a cruise. The child is very happy to see them, even though they cannot spend the night.

With the many guests gone and her sugar rush finally drained of power, Tressa Prophet quietly nods her way toward sleep. The door slides open, allowing a shaft of light to split her bedroom. Killian and Miranda come and sit on either side of Tressa's bed.

"Mommy, what's wrong?" the sleepy child asks.

"Nothing, Sweetheart. We just wanted to say night-night to our favorite girl."

Her drowsy eyes touch their souls as she says, "Thank you for my party. I never had so much fun."

Killian reaches into his shirt pocket. "Tressa, we saved the best present for last. We have one more gift for you."

"Really? Nothing could be better than Dancer, Daddy."

Her parents glance at one another. Then Killian says, "Oh? Well, then I suppose we saved the *second*-best for last." He places a gold bracelet around her left wrist and secures the clasp. "This is called a growth bracelet. Every year, as you grow bigger, we'll add another link to make it fit. Each link has a little charm on it. And each charm will remind you of how much we love you."

"Wherever you are, you can always look at it and remember that you're the brightest star that shines in our lives and we love you very much," Miranda adds. She hugs and kisses the sleepy child and leaves them alone.

Tressa sits up to place her arms around Killian's neck. With her eyes closed, she whispers, "I love you too, Daddy. Thank you for my bracelet and my puppy."

"You're very welcome, Tressa."

"Daddy?"

"Yes, Sweetheart?"

"Can Dancer sleep with me? He says his habitat is lonely when the lights go out."

Killian says, "So he can talk. What else has Mr. Dancer told you?"

She smiles with her head upon his strong shoulder. "Dancer says that he will be very quiet and he won't wet my bed. Promise."

Killian chuckles. As if the pup knows that they are discussing his sleeping arrangements, Dancer sits at attention. He tilts his head the way puppies do and whimpers softly. Killian lays Tressa upon her pillow, looks at the inquisitive Dalmatian and grunts. Dancer's tail thumps on the newspaper lining of the box as Killian reaches for him.

When he raises the puppy to eye level, Dancer cranes his neck to lick the writer's face.

"Okay, Dancer. My daughter, who is a very good judge of character, has vouched for you. Don't let us down."

Miranda's shadow moves down the hall as Killian places the puppy on the bed. Dancer licks Tressa's face, but she gets him settled beneath an arm before her father leaves.

Killian follows the west wind to their balcony, where his wife waits. They take a moment to look over the back yard and the dark, choppy waters of the Intracoastal Waterway and reflect on the very long day.

"I'm going to miss this place," Miranda says.

Killian sighs in reflection. "So will I, but our new home will bring new memories as our family grows."

"I took the test again today. I'm not pregnant, but soon."

He embraces Miranda and gazes into her eyes. "We've got time. Are you sure you don't want to wait until your new play has finished its run?"

"No way. The timing will never be right, so let's just go for it. As far as the play goes, I have the green light. Casting begins in two weeks, and I have complete autonomy. It's going to be quite a production, Mr. Prophet." Miranda smiles. "Oh, I forgot. While you were at the zoo, the inspector and contractor called. The property has been cleared for development, so I gave them the go-ahead."

"Really? Myrtle Beach, South Carolina, here we come," Killian says. "I love it when a plan comes together. I especially like having a wife who thinks and makes decisions on her own. Yes, Sir. I'm definitely the lucky one."

"Oh? You might not feel so lucky when I'm finished with you."

"Whatever do you mean, Mrs. Prophet?"

"You know what I mean," she says, arching her eyebrows. "Before starting the new book, you have a little more work to do because my loins are warm for you. Pleasure me, Husband." They kiss and go inside.

Four hours later, a boat drifts to the sea wall, where the occupants tie it fore and aft. They place rubber bumpers over the port-side railing to keep the wind from banging the boat against the concrete.

Three men dressed in black slither onto the shore. They are crouched low, crawling along the ground to reach the shadows of the home. Only then do they stand to check their weapons and proceed to break in.

With the plunger secured to the upper left corner of the door, the glasscutter efficiently carves a circular scar into the glass. The round section comes free with a little force. One of them uses a small mirror to look at the sensor inside. He reaches in with a small knife and deftly strips the plastic covering of the wires. A wire from his pouch is connected to them to insure the feed when the door is opened.

As the shorter man works on picking the deadbolt, the third person moves beneath the balcony. He sits to secure treeclimbing spikes to his boots. The other two are on the patio, moving slowly between the potted plants. They enter the foyer.

Killian has fallen asleep at his desk in the first-floor study. While he was on the tour to promote his latest work, a new novel had begun brewing in his head. He was anxious to get his thoughts down. Once he got started, he managed to shape its outline through the tenth chapter before drifting off. Satisfying his and Miranda's lust has taken something out of him, but his brain and fingers were all he needed to get this far on the new project.

The men are at the top of the stairs, checking every room. When the shorter one eases Tressa's door open, a pair of limegreen eyes at the child's side surprises him.

Dancer stands on four shaky legs, growling at the sweating intruder. The puppy shakes its head, bouncing once as it growls again. Tressa reaches for the pup, moaning her displeasure. Dancer begins to bark, despite her sleeping attempt to quiet him.

The intruder moves quickly, but he is too late. As he reaches for the retreating puppy, Tressa opens her eyes. He grabs Dancer by the nape of the neck and flings him toward the window. Tressa screams as the glass shatters. Dancer is falling to his death!

Killian awakens. The scream had not been a part of his dream. Using the key, he opens the gun cabinet and runs barefoot to the stairs.

The man grabs Tressa by the foot and drags her from the bed. She kicks him in the face and continues to scream for her parents. With one eye closed, he snatches her by the arm.

Miranda Prophet falls out of bed with the sheets tangled around her ankles. "I'm coming, Tressa!" she shouts while struggling to free herself. Armed only with a mother's instinct to protect her child, she stumbles toward the door. The third intruder is climbing over the balcony wall behind her.

The other intruder hears Miranda's cries, so he positions himself before the door of the master bedroom, waiting for it to fly open.

Killian reaches the top of the stairs, running with his weapon raised to fire. Just as he approaches his daughter's door, a masked gunman bursts through with Tressa struggling in his grasp. With no time to think, he fires at pointblank range.

The bullet hits this assailant just below the left collarbone, exploding through his spine to splatter his blood all over the wall. Tressa falls with him.

The taller man at the end of the hall turns quickly, bringing his gun to bear too late. Killian's Colt roars three more times, sending him to his death. As Miranda snatches at the bedroom door, an errant bullet obliterates the wood inches from her face, forcing the doorknob from her grasp.

Blood is everywhere. The man before her has fallen to his knees with his torso pressed against the wall to the left. He is dead, kneeling with his face pressed against the beige drywall. Miranda, frozen by a near miss, stares down the hall at her husband and frightened child.

As he takes Tressa in his left arm, Killian notices the flowing white curtains of the balcony behind his petrified wife.

When Killian realizes that another intruder has opened the door, he raises his gun and runs toward his wife.

"He's behind you. Get down, Miranda!" he shouted.

The shotgun roars. Holding a tight pattern at that short distance, the buckshot bores through Miranda Prophet's spine, each pellet slamming into the small of her back. There is a clatter as the expended shell makes room in the breach for another. Again, the shotgun roars.

Killian bellows, firing his gun as Miranda goes down. His bullets force the intruder backward as they hit him in the bulletproof vest. Blood explodes from the intruder's right shoulder just as he pulls the shotgun's trigger.

As Miranda goes to her knees, the upper part of her torso falls backward as the lower body bends forward. With her shoulders ending up between her ankles, she folds in half right before Killian's unbelieving eyes.

Killian's last two bullets hit the intruder in the chest and unprotected hip to drive him over the balcony. The shotgun goes off as the killer falls backward, its red-hot pellets ravaging both of Killian's thighs to send him crashing to the floor.

The wounded writer slides to a rest just outside his bedroom door. With searing pain racing through his legs and his dying wife folded before him, he still has the presence of mind to cover his daughter's face. Tressa is screaming as her father's hand moves to shutter her eyes.

Paralysis, like a creeping malignance, takes hold as Killian stares into Miranda's eyes. It travels from his toes to his burning eyes in a single heartbeat. The dying wife and loving mother strains to reach through merciless waves of pain, convulsing as blood seeps from her lips. As tears roll down her cheeks, Miranda Prophet whispers his name. Her eyes stretch as the world grows dim. Her silent lips open and shut.

The phone begins to ring. Sirens filled the air as security and police answer a neighbor's report of gunfire. Killian weeps, reaching for his broken wife. Miranda Prophet quivers once more, then she is gone, taking the greater part of his being with her.

Thirteen sullen months have passed. On the ground floor of the apartment that they took to be near their son, Tressa's grandparents are debating. The old house—where chalk outlines haunt the floor at Tressa's bedroom doorway and the wall and carpeting outside the master bedroom, like one-dimensional ghosts in stasis—is boarded up. The homicide investigation, while technically still open, is inactive. For the investigators, the trail just went cold.

Tressa has awakened early. The listless child sits quietly on her bed, taking no joy from her dolls while listening to the muffled voices of her grandparents, who are discussing her immediate future from opposite points of view.

Annoyed by his wife's pressing of the issue, Anders places his coffee cup on the kitchen counter. He says, "Doctor Mead said it's not good, Ethyl. Tressa has grown afraid of her father. Woman, why can't you accept that?"

Standing before the kitchen window, Ethyl Prophet turns on her husband with stern conviction in her squinting eyes.

"That woman doesn't know that Martin Luther King is dead. She has no children of her own, so her diplomas don't mean squat. Killy is trapped within himself, and Tressa is the only God-blessed thing left of his happy life. She's the only person that can save our son from this depression. I know it, Andy. I know it deep down in my bones. That child's the key to his recovery, not medicines or therapy."

"That may be, Ethyl, but Killian has rejected her. He's shut out the entire world, and Tressa is too young to feel anything other than fear. He's not the same person she knew. We should not force her to go back."

"We must, don't you see? Without her, Killian may never recover. Our grandchild is the only thing on God's green earth with the power to bring Killian back to the real world. I love Tressa with all my heart, and I wouldn't do anything to hurt her."

"But that's exactly what's going to happen if you force her to go back."

"What else can we do?" In frustration, Ethyl raises her trembling fists to the ceiling to declare, "Lord Jesus in heaven, tell me what we should do. What can we do, Lord? My son is so lost." Her stifled tears now flow freely, because she knows her husband is right.

Anders comes to her. His own eyes are welling when he whispers, "It's for the best, Ethyl. When Tressa is ready, she'll let us know."

Now a small voice comes from the doorway. "Grandma, is my daddy really in there? Is he really in there, Grandpa?"

Ethyl suddenly stiffens and wipes her tears away with her back turned. They go to the child, both feeling ashamed that she overheard their conversation.

Ethyl kneels, hugging their grandchild as Anders caresses her curly locks. The trusting child asks, "Is he, Grandma?"

Ethyl sniffles. "Yes, Baby, your father is in there."

"But he scares me," she whispers.

"I know, but he doesn't mean to. We're afraid, too, but he really doesn't mean it. Your father loves you very much, Tressa. He loved your mother, too, and it really hurt him when she died. It hurt your father so much that he ran away inside his own mind. Now he's simply lost. He wants to return, but he just doesn't know how to find his way back, that's all."

Tressa looks up to her grandfather, who smiles reassuringly. With compassion, the child wipes the tears from her grandma's cheek and says, "Then I want to see Daddy because he needs me."

Anders asks, "Are you sure, Tressa? We won't make you go if you're not ready."

"I'm sure, Grandpa," she says. "My daddy needs me now."

Ethyl hugs her. She looks upward, praying and thanking God in silence. Anders makes the phone call to inform Dr. Mead of Tressa's decision.

Dr. Andrea Mead and Killian's therapist meet with the grandparents to discuss what they are about to do. They have to make certain that the child's welfare comes first, that the decision has not been forced upon her.

Killian is sitting in his wheelchair before a large picture window. His limbs have healed completely, but he is a hair's breadth from comatose. This state of lethargy is all that he has known since his wife's death. He's been sitting there day after day, staring out at a white sheet of absolute nothingness, reacting to no stimuli or encouragement. No drugs could pull him from the abyss, where his body only takes the sustenance forced upon him through a tube.

With his face stubbly and withering, Killian blinks absently from time to time. His head tilts to the left, resting on the padded framework of the wheelchair as if he has not the will to lift his heavy thoughts.

The grandparents and doctors are standing near the doorway. Tressa Prophet crosses the room alone, taking tiny steps with her heart pounding in her ears.

Clasping the stem of a single daisy, she stands beside him with the afternoon sun creeping upon the windowsill. She stands there, looking at the very sad man she calls "Father." He seems so helplessly lost, buried under that suffocating mound of guilt.

Tressa whispers, "Daddy? It's me . . . Tressa. I miss you so much, and now I'm afraid you'll never come back to me. Please come back. Please, I need you." She glances at her grandmother in despair, but does not quit. "You have to come back now, or I will be all alone forever and ever, Daddy!"

Though Killian's expression shows no hint that he hears her plea, she offers him the flower. As her wrist enters the brilliant sunlight, her charmed bracelet captures its essence. It shimmers before Killian, touching his face with golden diamonds that play upon his skin and eyes.

A moment later, Tressa's watering eyes bulge, and tears began to flow down her glowing cheeks. Ethyl is disheartened and ashamed for having pressed the issue. She takes hasty steps toward the child, wanting to soothe Tressa's hurt. Halfway across the room, she freezes.

Tressa begins to smile at her father, who slowly raises his head to gaze upon the glistening gold bracelet. That shimmering talisman had been empowered by a purity of love that was rich when presented to the courageous child on her seventh birthday. It beckons him from the rift in which he has fallen. It seems to amplify her resounding words as they guide him back, and begin to mend his broken spirit. His twitching eyes slowly follow Tressa's forearm all the way to her trembling smile and hopeful eyes.

The child raises her arms, and Killian Prophet embraces her with all the strength he can summon from his weakened muscles.

Ethyl wilts to her knees to thank God, soon joined there by her husband. Killian finds freedom in the glow of Tressa's love where she stands in the doorway, welcoming him back from an undeserved hell. Yes, he finds freedom at last.

## CHAPTER 5

# Missy Ma'am

*Myrtle Beach, South Carolina*

Ethyl Prophet places her teacup on its saucer and wipes her cheeks. She says, "Now you know the whole story, Essie, what matters most."

Killian's neighbor politely wipes her hands with a napkin and says, "Wow. That horrible ordeal must have been very hard on all of you. I can see why your family has such a strong bond, especially between Killy and Tressa."

"This is true. On that terrible night, Killian saved Tressa's life. And then, when there seemed no other way on earth, she saved his," Ethyl says. "But what about you, Dear?"

Essie Dantzler asks, "Me? What do you mean, Mrs. Prophet? I mean, Ethyl. Sorry."

Ethyl reaches for Essie's hands, which are clasped about her knees. "Please pardon my intrusion. I'm just concerned. You are a self-made woman. You're strong, intelligent—and very beautiful, I might add."

Essie blushes. "Stop it, please. You're going to give me a swelled head."

"You have just about everything anyone could wish for in the world, but you have no one. I just think that it's so sad that you're alone."

"I appreciate your concern, but I'm okay, really. I'm happy. My life is my own again, and my business is thriving," Essie replies, knowing exactly where this conversation is going.

"There are often times when throwing oneself into one's work becomes an actual lifeline. Yet, it's also true that the very thing that saves us from the painful past often becomes our future prison. You are a lovely young woman, Essie, but working hard cannot fill the void forever, because there is so much more to life. When you're poor, broke and hungry, making ends meet can become the sole purpose of your existence. It's so sad when you've beaten the odds through hard work and dedication, but there's still no one there to share it."

"Oh, I see," Essie says coyly.

"When Killian returned to us, his sole inspiration was Tressa. His physical wounds had healed. When he finally left the hospital, we stopped at the cemetery where Miranda was laid to rest. I will never forget that dismal day. When we stopped the car along the drive, Killian got out alone. It was not until he knelt before Miranda's grave that we realized that no one had told him where she was buried. He seemed drawn to her grave by something that neither my husband nor I could explain. My son fell to his knees in the slush and rain and wept like a baby. Without warning, Tressa got out of the car and joined him there. She placed one hand upon her mother's gravestone and the other upon her father's shoulder. He hugged that child with all his might. After that day, Killian worked on getting his body back in shape, growing closer to Tressa with every passing moment. Then he began to write again, exercising his God-given talent. Once again, he threw himself into his work. When this house was finished, he moved to Myrtle Beach, which was very difficult to do. But he had to move on."

Essie says, "And now his life's complete."

"I thought so, at first. Then I realized that something was missing."

"Now just what could that be?"

"I've seen the way you two look at each other—and don't bother denying it, young lady," Ethyl says with a wicked little smile. "I see two lonely people, with very different pasts, finding themselves at the same crossroad in life, and I have to ask myself *why*? Why can't you two break through the barriers of the past to walk a mile together? Just a mile—that's all I ask."

Essie seems saddened. With her brown doe eyes seeking the window, she says, "I don't think Killian's ready for that, Ethyl.

For that matter, neither am I."

"Why do you say that?"

"Even though I loved him, my ex-husband really hurt me, Ethyl. He took so much out of me, things that I doubt I'll ever have again," Essie confesses. "I'm afraid, I suppose."

Ethyl wipes the woman's tears and smiles reassuringly. "I believe that you both are being offered that second chance, Sweetheart. If you can just find the courage to embrace it, I believe the entire world can be your Eden. It is no accident that God made the human heart the strongest muscle in the body. We gain strength through our adversities, just as long as we have the heart to reclaim ourselves from the ashes of shattered dreams and enormous disappointments. God made us this way because, like Him, we are conquerors. Trust me, Child—a mother knows these things."

A tall black man with dark glasses opens the door and peers in. When he clears the doorway, Tressa comes pouring through with a rottweiler puppy hot on her heels.

The happy nine-year-old runs directly to her grandmother.

When she sees Essie Dantzler sitting there, the child grins from ear to ear. She places her hands on her hips and wiggles when she says, "Hi there, Missy Ma'am."

Essie returns the smile. "Hello there, Missy Ma'am. I see you've decided which puppy you want to keep from the litter."

Dancer II sniffs at Essie's feet. Tressa scoops the heavy pup from the floor and says, "He's a good one."

Essie pets the puppy's soft coat. "He sure is, Missy Ma'am."

When Anders and Killian come in, Tressa puts the playful pup down and runs to her father. Dancer is in her wake, where he always seems to be. Anders sees her coming and volunteers to take their things upstairs, so Killian allows his daughter to lead him.

Looking up at her revitalized father with an enthusiastic smile, Tressa says, "Look who's here, Daddy. It's Essie!"

"I see," he says with his eyes upon the guest. As Tressa releases his hand to snuggle with her grandmother, he says to Essie, "Hey, you."

With a gleam in her eyes that she could not account for if asked, Essie Dantzler says, "Hey, yourself. I see someone's been shopping."

Killian smiles. "That little girl has impeccable taste, and more energy than ten men."

As Ethyl hugs Tressa, she watches their exchange. Her son has grieved long enough. And to her, he's done so more than most.

The loss and sadness had taken Killian Prophet to the edge of total oblivion. As any mother will, Ethyl wishes his rediscovery of that vital love. Essie Dantzler could be that love.

In a very subtle way, Ethyl and Tressa are in cahoots, but the child's enthusiasm for their neighbor is a bit less jaded.

Tressa's grandmother is satisfied, so she stands and pats her son on the shoulder to excuse herself. She leads Tressa to the kitchen, where Anders is munching on a freshly baked cookie.

With a few crumbs spilling into his palm, he says, "You've got that look in your eyes, Woman. You've been at it again— and don't you deny it."

Ethyl smiles innocently. "I've done nothing of the sort. I'm just watching nature take its course."

"More like helping nature along. I've known you much too long to buy that—even at a discount."

"You know, old man, you might be right about that. You should also know by now that I'll never admit guilt, which I learned from my husband."

With a warm cookie in her hand, Tressa asks, "What's nature?"

Just as the shocked grandparents glance at each other, Dancer slides into Anders's heel, attacking the hem of his slacks. The puppy gives the old man quite a start.

Ethyl says, "Ah. Nature is . . ."

Dancer growls and Anders grins at his wife's stumbling over the subject. "Well, Sweetheart, nature is sort of like what makes your puppy go after my pants."

"Oh. You mean he can't help it?"

With relief, Ethyl says, "Exactly. Ms. Essie and your father can't help liking each other."

They all laugh when the puppy growls and shakes the hem of the grandfather's pants from side to side. They will table the subject of matchmaking, for the moment.

"So how are you today, Mr. Prophet?" Essie asks.

While offering his hand, he says, "I'll tell you if you'll take a walk with me."

She accepts help to her feet. "Okay, but it will have to be a short walk. I'm showing Chuck Knoll's house this afternoon."

"Former Pittsburgh Steelers' Coach Chuck Knoll?"

"The one and only. He misses his parents' spread, so he's packing up and moving home."

"I'm happy to know it's not because I moved into the neighbor-hood," Killian says jokingly.

"Oh, I'm quite sure I wouldn't be handling this if he was that sort. Actually, he's a very personable man."

Three sets of eyes pop back into the kitchen as Killian and Essie approach. He stops at the control panel on the wall inside the kitchen, looking at his extremely innocent family with a very knowledgeable smirk upon his own face.

Killian hits a black button and says into the com panel, "Tija, come!" One of the kennel doors opens and Dancer's father trots out into the backyard.

Essie says, "Tressa, your father and I are going for a walk. Would you like to join us?"

Tressa smiles and looks up at her expressionless grandmother. She does not hesitate to say, "No, thank you. Grandma says I'm catching a cold, so I'm going to eat some chicken soup. Can you write me a rain check?"

Essie and Killian both chuckle. She says, "A rain check it is, Missy Ma'am."

"Lord, this child is too smart. What in the world does she know about rain checks?" Anders declares.

Killian notes the comical expression on his parents' faces. "That's pretty good. I mean, that's really good."

"Well, don't look at me," Ethyl says, unable to meet Killian's gaze with a straight face. When they turn toward the back doors, words cannot describe how proud Ethyl is of her grandchild.

As they exit, the powerful male Rottweiler heels obediently. Both adults greet Tija affectionately before strolling through the garden on their way to the beach.

With clouds closing in from the west, they stand at the water's edge, where Killian tosses a tennis ball. His dog eagerly gives chase down the beach.

One of the bodyguards stands atop the dune at the end of Killian's property. His alert eyes pivot from left to right, searching for anything amiss on the deserted beach.

"Your mother is incorrigible," Essie says, grinning.

"That she is," Killian agrees. "I'm afraid she's even recruited my daughter. Damn, she's good."

"Then we may not stand a chance, Killy."

They giggle as the dog returns with the tennis ball. "Are you going to be busy tonight?" he asks.

"What?" she asks, surprised. "Oh, I'm free after the Knoll estate. What do you have in mind?"

Killian's eyes are downcast, but hopeful. "Well, Ms. Dantzler, I suppose I'm asking if you'll have dinner with me tonight."

"I think I'd like that very much. What time should I come over?" she teases.

"Oh. I meant out, away from home."

"I know what you meant. I doubt that either of us could stand up to the combined forces of Ethyl and Tressa Prophet."

Killian is pleased that she accepts his unrehearsed invitation. They are both busy people and neither has dated in a very long while. They stop to gaze at the choppy Atlantic while its saline foam effervesces at their feet.

He sighs. "I like this place. I've always been drawn to the water."

"Same here, but we lived along the Hudson when I was growing up. It was a bit filthy then."

"Well, then it's settled. Tonight we will dine by the water. Do you have a preference?"

"Not really." She pauses. "Killian . . ."

He looks at her, hearing an important question in her voice. "Yes, Ms. Dantzler?"

". . . Are you sure about this?" she asks, looking away.

Essie feels inadequate, like used goods gone-sour, not quite good enough. Her past has dealt massive blows to her self-esteem, which she fears he will never fathom.

The bodyguard is now standing on the beach, facing the dunes with his legs apart and his hands clasped at his groin. The tall, bald man resembles a black stone pillar that has been erected during the night. This man is a professional. The principle is behind him with a special friend, staring out at the water in peace because of his presence.

Killian tosses the ball into the water. "It's just dinner. I'm sure that I want to eat, if that's what you mean."

"I meant . . ."

"Essie, I know what you meant," he says. "Just what has my mother been telling you?" His eyes are now searching the ocean waves for something he is not sure he will see.

The dog is swimming back.

"Everything. She finally told me the whole story."

He says, "I see." There is no particular inference on his words, no remorse or condemnation. "Then I should ask you the same question, Ms. Dantzler. Are you sure?"

She arches her eyebrow. "And just what has your mother told you?"

He smiles. "Everything I need to know. It seems that we both have issues and baggage. Some of it may be worse than many, but since we're both alive, we may as well live." Feeling an uncertainty in the very words he's just spoken, Killian adds, "Don't you think?"

Without thinking, she takes him by the arm. "That's really good. You should write that down, Mr. Prophet."

"Corny, huh?"

"But nonetheless true," she admits with an unusual sense of relief.

The wet dog decides to sling the water from its coat right in front of them. Caught off-guard, they run to avoid the spray.

It is time she leaves for her appointment. They part company on the beachfront by going to their respective landings, waving once more before disappearing from sight.

Nature is taking its course between this stunning woman and her handsome neighbor. Something deeper than their scars is growing. They still have barriers to cross, but not as mammoth as before. Though winter is fast approaching, the graying snow banks of their pasts are finally beginning to melt.

From his bedroom window, Killian watches as the Jaguar leaves her driveway. Essie Dantzler is a very intriguing woman. Her deep, soft eyes are rivers of thought. Though her spirit always seems chained within her, he sees more than hints of it in her glimmering eyes when she smiles. Moreover, her smiles are like gifts to him. She reminds Killian of Miranda, which he recognizes as part of the problem. He stands before that window, wondering why he just cannot . . .

Tressa pounces on him from behind, banishing the thought.

# That Feeling of Being Watched

*E*ssie Dantzler glances at the rearview mirror, trying to breathe normally. That feeling of being watched returns like hurricane winds, replacing recent vibrations of warmth with an irrational fear. It is crisp, this unshakeable burst of suspicion. Her ex-husband's recent release from prison is foremost in her mind. A condition of his parole prohibits him from seeking out or contacting his ex-wife. He supposedly has no way of knowing where she is, but a determined individual can find out such a thing with the help of the Internet.

With intent, an ordinary gray sedan cruises four car-lengths back. Tinted windows conceal the driver's identity.

When Essie parks in her designated place, she scans the immediate area for anything unusual. With her heart pounding, she pinches the bridge of her nose and inhales deeply to keep panic at bay. Despite herself, she recalls his fists pounding her. His spiteful words of vicious accusations resound from the walls of her mind. She relives being beaten into a stupor and waking several days later, greeted only by her own battered face in an ill-placed mirror. No friends, no family had come because they did not know. She was Jane Doe 21, and if she had died, she would have done so alone. Such are the involuntary thoughts of a battered wife. Essie tries to shake those powerful images, not noticing that someone approaches her car.

When that person bangs on the roof, she cries out. Terrified that he's found her, Essie grasps the steering wheel with both hands. She knows that the person beside her door is dressed in black, yet her eyes refuse to leave the windshield to face him.

Suddenly, a youthful smile appears before the windshield. Essie's heart gallops before recognizing her kid brother.

Her expression tells him that the prank had been ill timed. After three years, Latrell Dantzler thinks his sister has gotten over her abusive husband and is now free to appreciate a good scare. Sneaking up on her had been a terrible mistake, which becomes painfully clear when he looks into her terrified eyes. He remembers that Troy Whitman was recently released from prison.

She gets out of the car to hug her little brother, trembling all over.

"I'm so sorry, Essie. That was stupid of me," Latrell Dantzler says.

"Please don't ever do that to me again. Promise me that, Latrell. I almost pissed my fucking pants, you asshole!"

"I won't. I promise. That was inconsiderate of me. It'll never happen again. Am I forgiven, Big Sister?"

They end the long embrace. "Of course. I never could stay mad at you for long, now could I?"

"It's my boyish smile, isn't it?" he teases. "It'll get you every time."

She punches him on the arm. "What are you doing here? Why didn't you call to let me know that you were coming down?"

As they begin to walk toward the building, he says, "I missed you, so here I am. A couple of classes were canceled, so I figured I'd come down for a long weekend."

"I missed you, too. How's Mom?"

"She's fine." He notices the way she looks back at the parking lot as he opens the door.

"Where's your car, Latrell?" she asks.

He grimaces.

Two associates greet Essie. Her assistant announces that her three o'clock may be running a bit late, but they're on the way.

He waits until her secretary finishes speaking to say, "It died on the road. I had to have it towed a long way."

"Oh, I'm sorry. What's the matter with it?" she asks with genuine concern.

After they enter her office, he says, "Won't know until the mechanic gets to it tomorrow."

"You're going to be staying with me, right?" Essie asks.

"Well, actually, I was hoping you could lend me some money for a room."

"I see. So what's her name this time—Bambi? Or does it have more of a chocolate flavor, like Aquanetta Laquesha Monet? What?"

His blush is disingenuous. "Well, Big Sister, you know I don't kiss and tell. What kind of a guy do you take me for?"

"My whorish little brother. You'd better use protection, Latrell. The ninja kills people like you every day," she says while happily digging into her purse. "There's a new Budget Motel just a couple blocks from here. The rates are reasonable and the service is great. I send some of my out-of-town clients there. Give them this card and ask for the corporate rate." She gives him 200 dollars and her business card.

"Thanks, Essie."

"Oh, wait. Give your mechanic my number and I will take care of the repair costs. I can have Amy take you to get my wagon. Or stop by later to get it, if you like."

"Thanks again, Sis. I really appreciate this. I'll stop by tomorrow."

"I'm sorry that I can't spend any time with you right now. I have to meet a client soon and I kinda have plans for tonight. But I'll cancel that if you want," she says, almost hoping that he'll give her a reason to cancel the date with Killian.

"Oh snap, you've got a date? Hell no, don't cancel. You're too damn ugly to get another one anytime soon," Latrell says with a smile. "Poor guy. Is it due to an accident, or a birth defect?"

"What are you talking about?"

"His total blindness. Was it due to some terrible accident?"

"Ha, ha. That's very funny." Essie gives him a hug. "When Laquesha Monet is out of your system, I'd like you to spend part of the weekend with me. Promise?"

"You got it, big sister."

Her nostrils wrinkle. "And I'm sorry to tell you this, but you need to take a shower before going a-courting. Your new cologne is a bit nauseating. It reminds me of cat piss and onions."

The comment is treated as a joke, but quickly dispatched without retort.

As they embrace before the window, a telephoto lens captures Latrell Dantzler's image.

Several frames are taken as he exits the building. The lens disappears behind darkened windows.

Essie watches from her window as her brother enters a cab. She does not notice the gray sedan pulling away from the curb to follow, but the fine hairs on the nape of her neck are standing on end. She shivers and shakes it off.

When the clients arrive, she greets them with flawless grace.

Latrell's cab carries him to North Myrtle Beach where he stops at a Mom-and-Pop grocery store. The cabby waits out front, never to know that Latrell Dantzler has used the side door to an alley, where he buys crack cocaine from a dealer. However, the driver of the gray sedan watches his transaction, recording the exchange on film.

Ten minutes after Latrell goes into a less-than-ideal hotel, the private detective ventures inside. He uses false credentials and forty dollars to get the name of the young man who just registered.

Raymond Lampoon is tired and irritable from his last hour of surveillance. He leaves town, heading west. With the blessings of a certain sheriff, he has Latrell Dantzler's past investigated.

Lampoon believes he has everything he needs to satisfy his clients. The forty-nine-year-old private investigator will be happy to rid himself of this assignment. After one week and two cities, he is ready to go home.

Lampoon has been an honest man most of his life. After twenty years of service with the Conway Police Department, he retired at age forty. After taking a year off just to fish and enjoy retirement, he got restless. He started a private detective agency eight years ago, and continues to enjoy a lucrative livelihood that often forces him to trudge through the muck and mire of nasty divorces and custody battles that make him cringe.

About two years earlier, regrettably, Raymond Lampoon found himself caught up in the ugliest little drama of them all. Because of his initial involvement, he is now forced to play this hand to whatever end.

Having lost its appeal, he tosses the soggy stump of the cigar from the window.

The *Mystic Star* pulls away from the pier around seven. With the cooling night air frosting windows, there aren't very many people aboard the riverboat. As they cruise the Intracoastal Waterway, happy couples drink, eat and dance to their hearts' content.

Essie is wearing blue. She is perfectly stunning in a clinging dress that shows off her curves. Killian is wearing a tuxedo, something he usually avoids like the plague. Just as they agreed to play dress-up for this date, they decided on seafood, and the *Mystic Star* is reputed for its seafaring menu.

Essie's diamond necklace prompts Killian to say, "Tressa saved me when I was lost out there, wherever I had gone to."

"I imagine that your wife's death must have been extremely painful for you. I was once paralyzed, vegetating in front of that very same picture window . . . lost . . . dwindling, out of sorts with the rest of the world," Essie confesses. She shivers, but not from the weather.

Despite his apprehension, Killian says, "I'd like to find that we have more in common than pain and blank windows, where no living thing can thrive."

"So would I, Killy. I really would."

"I'm happy that we can finally talk about these things, and I thank you for all that you've done for my daughter and me, Essie. Your friendship is deeply appreciated."

He forces himself to reach out and touch her hand. With their fingers meshed, she says, "You're very welcome, but I haven't done anything."

"I beg to differ, Ms. Dantzler."

"You know, it is good we've had this talk, especially since you were so tight-lipped when we first met." She smiles. "You were really shy, Killy."

"Me?" he says. "You were the one who was afraid of her own shadow."

Her eyes suddenly lose their spark. Without realizing it, Essie withdraws. She looks away and begins to wrench her hands. Killian senses her distress, knowing that his last statement has resurrected dark and unpleasant memories. He wants to reach out again, but holds back.

"Would you care to talk about what's been bothering you?"

With a conscious effort, she stops her nervous hands. "My little brother popped up today."

"Really? I thought he was in college."

"He's got it good. His grades are up and he has the luxury of time and seniority, so he took a few days to visit his big sister. I suppose he's a bit concerned for me," she says, edging back toward a conversation she'd hoped to avoid. "Of course, he's got to get his freak on first. That's why he's nowhere to be found."

"You seem to be preoccupied lately. Yes, we're back to that. You know, you're very good at changing the subject. You're almost as good as my mother, but not quite. If you don't want to talk about it, I'll understand. If you do, I'm here for you.

"How very persistent of you, Mr. Prophet. It must run in the family."

"I don't mean to pry."

She takes a sip of wine and gazes out at the shimmering lights upon the water's surface. With a sigh, she says, "It's my ex-husband. He was paroled recently, and I guess I'm a little nervous."

"So you're afraid that he'll come looking for you."

"Yes," she confesses. "It was my testimony that put him away for what was supposed to be five years. That was three years ago. There was so much rage and utter contempt in his eyes as he vowed to get revenge."

Essie feels guilty for dumping this load on their first evening out. She jumps when a set of wine glasses crashes to the floor of the bar. While some of the other passengers applaud the mishap, she places her face in her hands.

Killian's hand moves toward her, stopping midway in a moment of uncertainty. "You really are scared. I understand your concerns, but it may never come to that. Instead of thinking that he has spent the last three years plotting his revenge, maybe he's come to realize that he belonged there for what he did to you. It's called 'reform.' Then again, he may have dropped his vendetta all together. Besides that fact, he has no idea where you are. I'm sure that no one in your circle of family or friends will ever tell him. Also, there could be another important consideration."

"What's that?" she asks.

"He might be wearing a pink dress and makeup now."

They burst into laughter. Killian holds out his hand and lets his wrist go limp to drive her over the edge. Essie was taken totally by surprise.

Moments later, she says, "Maybe you're right."

"I'm almost always right. You'll see," he says with a sincere smile.

"It's just that, lately, I've had such an intense feeling that I'm being watched. It's silly, right?"

Killian looks at her seriously for a moment. Then he says, "Not at all. To tell the truth, I've been experiencing the same thing. I know that sudden, unreasonably panicked burst of adrenaline well. Believe me."

"Maybe we're both a couple of paranoid schizophrenics."

"Shhhh!" he cautions while looking about as if he has something to hide. "Please don't say that too loudly. We should try to keep that little observation to ourselves, because you never know when they may be listening."

The giggle is a relief for them both. However, Essie feels the need to be held, and the only way she will feel comfortable is to ask if he'd like to dance. Killian is willing.

They end the evening with another walk on the beach, hardly noticing the bodyguard who tags along at a discrete distance. One of them always remains at home with Tressa when Killian is away.

The bodyguards are quite expensive, but his tragedy had also become a financial blessing in disguise. Killian's popularity as a writer soared while hospitalized. When he finally returned to the world, his agent was pleased to tell him that he was richer than he could ever have imagined. It was a macabre scenario— people wanting to know what he might have written that could piss someone off enough to kill. Killian experienced enormous guilt because he knew that the greater success had much to do with Miranda's murder.

After their walk, Essie Dantzler enters her home by the backdoor. As she stands in the kitchen, she catches her reflection in the black surface of the refrigerator. The single yellow rose is sweet to her nostrils, bringing a girlish smile to her lips.

Now there is a knock at the backdoor. Her heart flutters when she sees Killian's smile between the curtains. She quickly opens the door and asks, "Killy, is something wrong?"

"Yes." His eyes are intense. His smile becomes something more serious as he takes Essie by the hands and says, "I just forgot something."

He comes closer, gazing into her eyes with a secret desire pounding in his chest. She knows what he means to do, feeling only a momentary fear.

Gently, Killian takes Essie's face in his hands. He inhales her scent as their lips meet. Both hearts rage, pounding out a message like African drums across a sun-drenched savannah.

They moan in unison just before their lips part to give way to another kind of kiss. Her eyes open and rise to meet his, but no words are spoken until he backs away. For an instant, all of time and space seems to lapse into a gentle slumber, where the only sound in the universe is the steady rhythm of their hearts.

Killian's eyes are dancing with the playful flicker they had lost for so long. "I forgot to kiss you goodnight, Ms. Dantzler. But if you're no longer repulsed by me, I'll never forget again."

She blushes, secretly wishing for more. As Killian closes the door, he glances back at Essie Dantzler with a smile.

Long after he is gone, Essie still feels Killian's lips upon her own.

CHAPTER 7

# Gone in the Night

They have watched those flickering lighters nearly all night. Because the sun will be coming up soon, they can afford to wait no longer.

Before leaving the surveillance vehicle, they transform by putting on dark blue windbreakers that have "POLICE" embossed in yellow lettering on the chest and back. Bogus badges are clearly on display, hanging from their necks.

They boldly enter through the front door of the hotel, wearing black ski masks. Only the eyes and a little of their cheekbones are exposed. With weapons drawn, one of them places a finger over his lips to quiet the startled night clerk, who gives up the key and quickly hides under the desk in the office. The clerk has no desire to witness the arrest, knowing that this raunchy motel caters to many unsavory types, including gun-slinging drug dealers and users. He's seen men shot in this place, and police raids can be especially violent occasions.

As their arcane eyes peer at him through the cracked door, the pungency of burnt cocaine causes their nostrils to wrinkle in disgust. The nauseating odor is prevalent, as if he is still smoking. They slip into the room. Their target is lying on his stomach in a pool of sweat, oblivious to the same world that frightened him with so many suspicious sounds not long before. Ordinarily he would be wide awake, but the liquor and sleeping pills had effectively brought him down.

Something clatters on the bathroom floor. One of the intruders closes on Latrell's position while the other moves toward the door.

When the paranoid woman in the bathroom hears a noise, the hot lighter falls from her hand and skips across the chipped tile floor. Earlier, when Latrell wasn't paying attention, she cuffed some of his drugs. Now she thinks she's been caught. When the woman gets down on the bathroom floor to peek under the door, she expects to see his bare feet or his shadow. What she sees are the two sets of boots of the slow-moving men who just entered the room. One of them is now moving toward the bathroom.

The woman is panicked and trapped. Her stammering heart triple times it on its way to cardiac arrest. She looks about the tiny room and bolts for the window, tearing out the old slats of glass two at a time.

When the doorknob jiggles, she drops one of the glass slats and screams. As the door flies open, she slides into the darkness, wearing nothing but her bra and panties.

The shattering glass causes Latrell to stir. The presence of two masked intruders startles him. Before he cries out, the butt of a gun slams him back to sleep.

It has gotten cold. The death of fall has opened its doors to blustery winter winds. Icy drafts find their way through every nook and cranny of the alien boathouse.

Migratory fish are swimming south to flee the cooling, brackish waters of the Waccamaw River, taking the Intracoastal Waterway to the salty Atlantic.

A useless shutter taps against the wall where Latrell Dantzler lays shivering and bound. Three of his front teeth have been shattered. Two more are missing, gone forever. His severely chapped lips are busted and swollen. Anchored by fine hairs, clots of blood now block his nostrils and cling to a damaged left eye that oozes pus.

With torturous passion, what seems like a million needles now prick him relentlessly from within. Misshapen red blood cells are now jammed in his blood vessels like salmon swimming upstream against the raging current of a narrow passage. His nearly useless muscles are starving for oxygen, pleading as pain racks his body to make him twitch.

Latrell Dantzler now lies on the cusp of unconsciousness, trapped in a chilly environment that anyone with Sickle Cell Anemia knows well to avoid. Handcuffs about his wrists and shackles around his ankles are like ice clamps, a cold burning that is unrelenting. For him, this is truly unbearable.

With his bruised face pressed against the splintered floor, Latrell Dantzler whimpers, "Somebody, please help me. Help me."

Abducted in the early hours just before dawn, he was handcuffed and gagged before being dragged down the hall of his low-budget motel. His captors were dressed as police officers, but their method of arrest and treatment of this prisoner were crude and barbaric.

As Latrell Dantzler lies on the creaking floor of the boathouse, he cannot help recalling his sins, reliving his lies and theft. Once more, his waning consciousness replays his most recent transgressions.

During his first night in Myrtle Beach, Latrell spent his sister's hard-earned money on drugs and booze, taking a handsome whore for the night. She was just a local streetwalker who often failed to answer to one of her made-up names. When approached by the good-looking stranger, she was most eager to get out of the weather. She seemed healthy enough, though a little rundown down by the life. Her former beauty was winding down like a tired battery in a twenty-nine-year-old clock. Before taking a shower, she smelled of old sex, sweat, and smoke. The blond hooker was destined to be Latrell's queen for a day at his sister's expense. Once he got started, it was hard to stop. Because he needed more, the creative mind began to spin lies at light speed.

The whore had called Essie's office on the following day, pretending to be the secretary of some nonexistent auto mechanic. With Latrell's guidance, she explained to Essie that Latrell had blown the engine in the car. The mechanic just happened to have a replacement and was willing to install it for a mere 2,600 dollars. The cost would cover parts and labor. The work would come with a warranty, of course.

Essie had agreed, giving them authorization to begin the work. The secretary informed, however, that her company only accepted cash for jobs on out-of-state automobiles. The policy stood, regardless of who paid the bill. They would not accept a check or credit card for such substantial work. Naively, Essie agreed to the terms, promising that her brother would have no problem raising the cash.

Twenty minutes after the call, a tired looking Latrell Dantzler showed up to hear the bad news about a car that he'd already sold for drugs in New York. Because Essie was expecting an important client, she could not drive him all the way to the garage. It saved Latrell the trouble of inventing a viable excuse to dissuade her further involvement.

Essie also threw in money for cab fare and expenses, again offering the use of her station wagon for the duration of his stay. He could even drive it back to New York until his car was ready, or she would spring for a plane ticket.

After a trip to Essie's bank, Latrell returned to his hovel and spent her money as if it was a rich man's pocket change. Though he knew she loved him dearly, he was burning bridges with impunity, knowing that the ugly day of reckoning may lie just around the dawning bend. Yet his addiction had him convinced that it was worth it.

This young man had done all of those things without knowing that two men would ease into his bedchamber to snatch him from the air. That, however, was nearly two weeks ago.

During the earlier days of captivity, he'd lived on bread and water, consuming both as if he was an animal. However, the cold and pain have now stolen his appetite, taxing his very will to live.

Moss-laden trees stand as sentries along the gravel road to the boat landing. There is about a hundred yards between the river and the house, which stands three stories high. This estate is serene and timeless.

From the top floor, facing east, one can see a great distance across a marshland that's now deserted by most of the indigenous waterfowl.

The plantation house is quiet. Retired Judge Barnes sits in a wooden wheelchair, though fully recovered from the stroke that had nearly taken him to join his youngest son in hell.

Judge Barnes has moved away from the dining room table, where his eldest son, Sheriff Roscoe Barnes, discusses the next phase of a fiendish plan with those who actually snatched Latrell Dantzler from the Beachcomber Hotel.

With the light fading in the parlor, Sheriff Barnes turns on the hanging lamp to illuminate the table as he passes photos to Officer Baker.

Officer Baker gives a quick glance at the sheriff's fidgety younger brother, the third man at the table. "The parents live alone," Sheriff Barnes says while rubbing an aching shoulder. "The address is on the back. Neighbors are sparse and well spaced, so it should be relatively easy to get in and out. Just make sure you leave at least one of them alive. Is that clear, Baker?"

Officer Baker, a burly specimen whose girth is straining his waistband, grunts but says nothing while perusing photos taken two weeks ago by Ray Lampoon.

After hours of preparation, Sheriff Barnes says, "Hit them fast and hard."

CHAPTER 8

# Departure

*K*illian and Essie are sitting in the den, giving little notice to a predicted drop in temperature in the days to come. With a menacing cold front moving in, there was even a chance of early December snow.

He reaches for her hand as she gazes at the flickering fireplace. Essie smiles at Killian's touch, but her eyes are plagued with sadness. This profoundly deep melancholy is filled with foreboding thoughts.

"Your brother may pop up at any minute. I pulled something similar when I was his age. After all is said and done, you'll probably find that a girl's behind his sudden disappearance. You'll see," Killian says, hoping to give her something to cling to. Of course, his reassurance is consistent with Essie's previous description of Latrell's energetic sex life.

"I haven't been very good company tonight. I'm so sorry, Killy."

"Not at all. Even though I'm an only child, I can still feel what you're going through. I'm just trying to think positively, Ms. Dantzler."

"It's just that Latrell has never completely disappeared. Not like this. He would always let my mother know where he would be going, or how he could be reached. I just have a bad feeling about this. It has been far too long."

"Are you certain that he's never gone AWOL?"

"Never like this. He's a responsible young man, maybe wild at times, but responsible. My mother has been worried sick since he failed to show up in New York. I swear to God, that boy is going to answer for this."

"Has your mom gotten any sleep since she arrived?" he asked.

"I had to convince her to take one of my sleeping pills, so she's gotten some rest in the last two days. I'm afraid that she'll stop taking them. You know how old people are about taking narcotics and their taboos against drug addiction."

"This is true."

"Good Lord in heaven, you should have seen the look that woman gave me when I suggested she take that pill. You'd think I'd suddenly gone insane, but she finally came around to my way of thinking."

"Like pulling teeth without anesthetic," he replies.

Essie smiles genuinely. "Do you know what I said to finally get her to take them?"

"What?"

"'Mother, remember what you used to say when I'd fight sleep on Christmas Eve? "Young lady, you're just afraid that you will miss something important. If you don't get some rest soon, you probably will miss out on exactly what you've been waiting for."'"

Killian grunts. "That's what my mother used to say to me and my cousins when we were growing up."

"It's amazing how people who've never met can have the same philosophy," she says.

"This is true. It's also true that young men are led around by the southern portion of their anatomies. Latrell probably fell in lust with some little firecracker that rocked his world, so he left the planet. He'll be okay."

"You're probably right."

"Of course I am. When you see him again, you'll give him a big hug and kiss. And then . . ."

"And then I'm going to wring his freaking neck. That's what I'll do, and you can help." They laugh.

She squeezes his hand. "Thanks, Killy. You've helped me a lot through this mess. I hope that I can return the favor someday."

He embraces her. "Just seeing the sun come out in your smile is thanks enough, Essie."

She squints. "Ooh. Now, you really should write that one down. I've been so self-absorbed of late that I forgot to ask how the new nanny is working out."

"Fine. Tressa likes her, and that's what counts," he says.

What's that accent?" Essie asked.

"She's originally from the Dominican Republic. She's been in the states for almost four years, but that thick accent may never fade completely."

"That's probably why Tressa likes her so much. She's having fun trying to figure out what the sister is saying." He laughs. "You know, I actually believe that I'm just a little jealous of her."

"I don't think you have to worry. Tressa likes her, but my little girl really cares for you, Missy Ma'am."

As if on cue, Erica Borja comes downstairs with a suitcase. She seems distraught, distracted as she wrings her hands. She places her things to the side and approaches the den, where one of her nicest employers sits with his female friend.

When Killian sees Erica's expression, he braces for bad news and excuses himself at her request.

Essie watches as they speak quietly in the other room. By Killian's reaction, the news is not good.

Prophet walks away. During his brief absence, Essie's eyes meet with those of the nanny. Just before the woman averts her eyes in shame, Essie discerns, with some acuity, a measure of fear. Perhaps she is afraid of Killian's wrath, expecting him to rant and rave at her and the agency that recommended her for this job.

When her employer returns, he gives her a check. She puts it in her purse, apologizing again for the inconvenience.

As she walks toward her suitcase and the door, Killian raises his palms to his face. With his eyes closed, he walks a tight circle of frustration. When the door closes behind Tressa's caregiver, Killian moves out of sight.

Essie is concerned and joins him in the office. He leaves a message for the agency that placed Ms. Borja nearly three weeks ago.

"Did she just quit on you?"

Killian sighs long and hard as he sits behind his desk. "She just up and quit. Just like that. Fuck!"

"I thought things were working out. Why would she leave so suddenly?" Essie asks as she crosses the room and takes a seat.

Killian's eyes seek the window and the light beyond the panes. "I suppose I can't really hold it against the woman because she just found out that she's pregnant. She talked to her boyfriend, who expressed concerns about her working in an environment that requires bodyguards." He inhales deeply and taps a manicured nail on the desktop. "Well, at least she gets a wedding ring out of the deal."

"Because she's pregnant, you didn't try to change her mind or rake her over the coals. That's commendable of you, Mr. Prophet. I, on the other hand, would have cursed that bitch to infinity and beyond. Well . . . maybe."

"I'm scheduled to leave for Washington tomorrow, and she pulls out on me at the last possible moment. Her biological clock couldn't have worse timing."

"What will you do now?"

"I may have to cancel the promotion of my new book. After all their time and preparations, Margo and my publicist are going to want my head. I suppose I could leave Tressa in Mason's care, but she still has a cold, as you know. I wouldn't be comfortable with that. My parents won't be back from Florida until day after tomorrow. I can take her with me and leave her with one of the hotel's nannies, but I'd rather not take her out in this weather with that cold. I really don't have much of a choice."

"I see your dilemma. It's a heifer, but not insurmountable."

"Do you want to know the worst part of it? I was just beginning to question my continuing need for the bodyguards. Hell, I stopped carrying my gun a long time ago. Now, this shit."

Killian places his fingertips on his pulsing temples and flexes his jaws in disgust. Tressa had been especially excited, looking forward to her father launching a new book and solidifying his reunion with his former life. However, her care comes first.

Calling Margo First, his literary agent, is a task he dreads, because his publisher contracted her to oversee the scheduling of this new tour on a trial basis.

Killian is so deep in thought that he does not notice that Essie has left her seat. Her soft hands caress his shoulders, causing the short hairs of his neck to bristle. Her soft-spoken words are meant to soothe Killian as she says, "I can keep Tressa. Leave her with me. It's only three days, and it wouldn't be a bother."

As she comes around the chair, he looks at her smile and considers the offer. "I couldn't do that to you and your mother, Essie. You've got enough trouble without having to look after my little monster."

Her eyes sadden for a moment, but she quickly resurrects her dazzling smile to say, "Tressa will be a welcome distraction for my mother and me. Besides, it would be my pleasure to care for the child of the man that I think . . . I love. And I do believe I have fallen in love with you, Killian."

Almost as a reflex, Killian rises. "What did you just say?"

Essie blushes. "Don't look so surprised, Mr. Prophet." She gazes deeply into his eyes, wanting more than words to pass between them.

Their eyes connect in a sensual, wordless embrace. As Killian holds Essie in his arms, he feels her heart pounding in her breast. Her racing pulse and a single tear from those fathomless doe eyes tell him that it has taken great effort to summon such meaningful words. It is a declaration that Essie Dantzler's heart now heeds, something more powerful than fear and loneliness in a world where sorrow once flourished.

For a moment of inexplicable doubt, they both tear themselves away from that gaze. But their eyes are quickly drawn back to the center of their longing.

Killian Prophet is compelled to respond to the confession, but he is not allowed to utter the words because Essie places her fingers over his lips.

"Shhhh. You needn't say it, Killy. I know what you feel for me because I'm surrounded by it whenever you're near me. I can almost smell it when we're in the same room. I hear it in your voice and words of comfort." Her eyes well up, spilling onto her smiling cheeks. "I can even taste it in your kiss."

Their lips meet in the twelfth hour, just as midnight chimes. When their burning lips finally part, Essie takes him by the hand and leads him to the stairway.

They make love for the first time, taking sustenance and pleasure as needed from bone-deep inner animals that move forward unto the approaching hours of dawn. With the power of this turning of a page, which signifies the closing of the old and the opening of new chapters in life, both will shed silent tears. Now, sleep is welcomed. Now sleep is the sweetest companion.

Tressa awakens around 8 a.m. She still has the sniffles and a slight cough, but she's beginning to feel better. The nine-year-old is a little disappointed when she peers into her dad's bedroom, but her eyes glisten when Essie moves. She is there, sleeping peacefully in her father's arms.

She runs to the phone to call her grandmother. It takes a moment to get through, but Ethyl finally answers. Evidently, nature is taking its course, which is expressed to Ethyl from the refreshingly innocent viewpoint of a child. Christmas and Santa Claus never delivered a gift so grand.

Tressa's father is complete. Ethyl Prophet's son is a whole man again.

<br />

CHAPTER 9

# *The Signing*

A stiff northwesterly wind blows from the Chesapeake as a strong cold front moves quickly across the Southeast.

The old woman is dreaming. Outside, the wind causes a vibration from that loose board on the eave, which her husband has sworn to fix this morning. The sound of it becomes a part of her dream, or it may have even caused the dream in which her father is repairing the tin roof of her childhood home. She is only eleven years old while standing below, looking up at him with the sun in her eyes. The breeze is warm but gusting. She is holding a glass of lemonade, smiling when he finally takes a break to have a drink beneath the hot Virginia sun.

The back door opens on well-oiled hinges that do not warn of the lone intruder. Before entering, Officer Baker glances over his

<br />

shoulder. Satisfied that no one sees him, he shuts the door and takes a butcher's knife from the cutlery set on the kitchen counter.

The stainless steel blade glistens in the dim light of the stairway, calling for blood to sate its metallic thirst.

Baker hears running water and follows the sound to the room at the end of the hall. Standing over her, as if he has absolutely nothing to fear, Baker watches as the old woman sleeps.

When the unfamiliar smell of depilatory offends Baker's nostrils, he looks at the bathroom door. The old man is in there shaving with that foul-smelling stuff.

The husband of forty years rinses his face in the sink. With his smooth face buried in a scalding towel, he hums an old song from the sixties.

When his eyes refocus, his murderer is staring back at him with a wicked glare. A gloved hand muffles the old man's cry a split second before the blade is driven into his back. The killer pivots, shifting his weight to the right while forcing the horizontal blade to slice through the retired cop's heart and left lung. His white tee-shirt is drenched red. When the killer snatches the hand from the old man's lips, blood spurts on the mirror to stain his unbelieving eyes. The old man slumps to the floor and convulses to his death.

A horrified scream suddenly fills the air when his wife surprises the murderer. She stares down at her husband sprawled at the feet of a killer with a bloody blade in his hand. This man's eyes are cold, revealing no remorse for his fresh kill, so she bolts. But before the woman makes it to her bedroom door, the knife is jammed into her right shoulder.

The screeching old woman falls, reaching for the haft, to no avail. She crawls down the hall with white-hot agony searing her body.

Her forward motion causes the blade to cut crooked grooves into the hardwood floor before snapping off at the tip. Through blurring vision and grinding teeth she struggles, on the verge of passing out.

The old woman knows that he will soon be upon her. When Baker rips the blade from her body, she screams. It is driven into her once more.

Thirty minutes later, with her husband dead and their home burglarized, she drags herself from the front door. The phone lines have been yanked from the wall. A mail carrier finds her a bloody mess and barely alive.

At either side of Barnes and Noble's entrance, there are poster-board photos of Killian Prophet holding a copy of his latest book. He is not smiling. His eyes are intense and serious.

CityCenterDC Mall is bustling. Killian is dressed in black slacks and a turtleneck. He sips from a glass of wine while looking down at the busy mall. A long line has formed while he replays scenes from Miranda Prophet's life before and after they were married.

Margo First walks in, knowing that Killian would be before that window.

This fifty-three-year-old woman is confident and alive. Her short blonde hair looks especially nice for this occasion. She has gone all out for this event, spending a mint on an original Versace business suit that carves ten pounds and years from her figure.

She joins him there to place her wine glass against his own, listening for that satisfying ping. Neither of them likes champagne, so wine it is. With a smile of satisfaction and anticipation, her blue eyes flirt with him.

"You know, I never realized just how good looking you really are. Maybe I should further inspect the goods," Margo says while looking Killian up and down with a raised eyebrow. "Are you ready to face your adoring public, Handsome?"

His hesitation causes her heart to flutter in the face of potential disaster. Then he smiles at her. "Got you, didn't I?"

As Margo shakes a benign finger at him, she says, "You're so bad. Are you trying to give me a heart attack?"

"Just a little one."

She takes the author by the arm and faces the window. "This is once again the window to the future," she says. "They love your work, Killian. The literary world has missed you." Margo's sigh is one of contentment. "And I, the woman who shall be known as the greatest literary agent in the world, will guide you to them once again. Are you ready, Mr. Prophet? Are those juices churning deep down inside?"

Killian returns the smile and confesses, "It's a little overwhelming, Great One. Hell—I'm shaking like a scared turtle on I-95 during a holiday weekend."

"So you finally agree that I, and I alone, am the indelible, undisputed reigning queen of all that you now see." She looks up at him. "Other than all that, I know that you can ride this bike again. You'll dazzle them just like you used to, Kiddo."

"There are a lot of people down there, Great One, and I feel like I'm about to bust wide open," he confesses.

"You're trembling," Margo observes. After he puts his blazer on, she helps straighten his lapel like a mother on her son's prom night. "Listen to me. This is a new beginning all around. I've noticed a fire in your eyes which usually only equates to having a new love in your life. I don't need my psychic abilities to see that, because I have two grown sons. I easily recognized that look when I caught you daydreaming earlier. Men don't smile that particular smile unless a woman's involved."

Killian blushes. "As my father would say to my mom, mind your own business, Woman."

Margo laughs. "See, there it is again. This is your first nonfiction project, your life story. Hell, you're not even forty yet. Look at them, waiting down there as if your signature were gold. Take my advice and enjoy yourself today, Killian. I know you well enough to know that you're feeling a bit guilty, but you shouldn't. I believe Miranda is up there pulling for you and Tressa. She wants you to go on with your life. She wants you to raise Tressa with someone you love, trust and respect, because she of all people knows that life's too short for so much guilt."

"Using your psychic powers again?"

"Listen to me now. Just listen. I felt so lost and so responsible when my husband died during our divorce proceedings. I could hardly get out of bed in the mornings following Miller's death. My work seemed to be the only thing that saved me from the depression, because people were depending on me. I couldn't afford to be depressed for long. I got back out there and made some things happen, but I found that it really wasn't enough. Now that I'm in love again, all is right with the world—just as it should be for you. Live, Killy. Breathe again. Fly with your heart wherever it soars—as long as it's not away from your writing."

"Amen, Sister. Preach that message."

"I'm serious, my friend. You once wrote that the closing of one chapter brings about the inevitable opening of another, even if it's a different book." Margo points down below. "Those people, and many more, want to believe that no matter what happens in their lives, things are going to be all right. You have given them that hope by just coming here, Killian. Those are not just your fans; they are your extended family. To some degree, they've all felt your pain, but now they rejoice in your return. You have become more than just an entertaining writer when total strangers begin to include you in their prayers, my friend."

Killian looks into his agent's eyes. With a smile that seems more thoughtful than before, he says, "I see you're also the greatest motivational speaker in the world. Thank you, Margo. I probably needed to hear everything you just said. Thanks."

"You're going to do just fine." She embraces him. They set the wine glasses on the ledge and walk out together. As they approach the door, Killian asks, "Before the conversation turned all serious, were you flirting with me? You were, weren't you? As your friend, Margo, I must warn you that jungle fever will probably kill you at your age. Although I'm flattered, I am involved at the moment. However, if you really insist on indulging your naughty little fantasy, I believe one of my bodyguards is single."

The feisty Philadelphian pretends to be shocked. She smiles, reaching back to pinch him on the ass. "How do you know my new boyfriend isn't black?" she asks.

They laugh as they approach the circular stairwell. As they descend, the applause and cheers prove her right. *Remembrance* is a success, and Miranda Prophet would be proud.

Hours later, after short breaks, the bodyguard notices someone among the autograph seekers and well-wishers. This person seems to be extremely anxious. His pensive eyes have been darting about as if expecting childhood monsters to pounce from shadows privy only to himself.

The bodyguard watches him from behind dark glasses, inching his way closer while waiting to see what this man will do when his turn comes. Noticeably, he does not engage in any of the usual small talk between perfect strangers. Among them, he is alone.

Killian glances at his bodyguard several times during his sessions. Now he notices that his protector has zeroed in on this man in particular, flanking discretely.

The man in the line is dressed in khaki pants, wearing a flannel jacket over his tee-shirt. The right sleeve of his thin jacket is rolled up to the elbow. He is carrying a copy of Killian's novel and a suspicious paper bag.

The writer's heart quickens when this supposed fan finally steps to the table. "Mr. Prophet, my name is Aaron Thomson, and I'd like you to autograph my book," he says politely. He is sweating and scratching himself absently. The depth of his nervous energy seems unfathomable in a moment of contagious tension. "My wife died last month, so I'd like you to make it out to her. Her name is Patricia—Patricia Thomson."

The bodyguard moves closer to the man whose dead wife could apparently read. The writer clears his throat, trying to dislodge the lump that has risen there. "You have my condolences, Mr. Thomson. I'm very sorry for your loss."

Killian's right hand moves through the inscription, but his eyes keep darting back to the person before him. The writer is paralyzed when Thomson reaches into his jacket.

"Thank you, Mr. Prophet. Before Pat died, she wanted me to give you something to remember us by." He yanks something from his inner pocket.

The bodyguard moves in, seizing Thomson's left wrist. When he clamps down on Thomson's neck with his right hand, Thomson is driven forward and pinned against the table. People in the line gasp in fear.

A camera crew is in the mall, just outside of the bookstore. They are interviewing those who have gotten books signed by a man once known as the Black Assassin. As frightened people begin to scramble for safety, they take notice.

The brown paper bag is torn, spilling three large pill bottles that roll across the blotter while autograph seekers scatter for cover. Many of them rush the exit to observe from a safer vantage point.

A rectangular black box comes to rest before Killian, who snatches it open despite his bodyguard's warning not to touch it. Killian's eyes bulge and his heart sinks.

Mr. Thomson protests, but he does not struggle. Killian places a hand on Mason's arm to call him off. He turns the box around and rises to apologize. Thomson is released immediately.

"It's okay," Aaron Thomson says. "I understand, Mr. Prophet. It was my fault. I meant no harm."

"Are you all right, Sir?" Killian asks as the bodyguard backs away, leaving him to make the apologies. "I'm terribly sorry. It's just that . . ."

Surprisingly, Thomson shrugs it off. "No harm done. I shouldn't have approached you that way." Thomson runs his fingers through his damp hair. As Thomson collects his meds, he clears his throat with downcast eyes. "This pen has been in Patricia's family for ten generations. It's made of solid gold, not plated. She made me promise to give it to you in case she wasn't here to see this day. There's an inscription. See? It says: 'In the hope that you may someday write the world a better place.'"

As his fans begin to return from whence they fled, Killian examines the pen. He says, "This is awfully nice of you and your wife, Mr. Thomson, but I couldn't accept such an extravagant gift."

Thomson is visibly disheartened, his eyes wilting in despair. They water as he says, "Please, Mr. Prophet. It was Patty's dying wish that I do this one thing right. She wished she could be here to extend an olive branch to apologize for what some very misguided members of our society have done to your lovely family. Please allow me to keep my promise, because it is also my own dying wish. Please accept this gift. That's all I ask."

Just as mall security personnel rush in, Killian comes around the table to embrace the AIDS victim. Margo rejoins them while the bodyguard speaks to the slow security guards, who were caught out of their designated positions.

The returning fans begin to applaud the inspirational acts of compassion. Tears are flowing down many cheeks. For both Killian Prophet and Aaron Thomson, they are tears of appreciation and grief that have finally been released.

Upon leaving, Mr. Thomson is harassed by reporters. He is soon approached by a lawyer, but will decline the chance to file a civil suit.

Mason's phone rings as he observes that vulgar display. The bodyguard moves away to take the call, keeping a watchful eye on his principal. He begins to pace.

Seconds after his brother's disturbing call, he is gone with Killian's blessing. Margo First makes sure that mall security maintains a presence.

Mason's parents are the unfortunate victims of an apparent robbery that turned violent. His brother told him their father was killed in the attack, but their mother lapsed into a coma after hours of surgery.

Margo is concerned for Killian's frame of mind. During the break, she finds him sitting behind the desk, considering the business card of the Principal One Personal Protection Agency. She takes the card from his fingers and asks, "Would you like me to request immediate replacements?"

To her surprise, he shakes his head to the contrary, though dubiously. "Do you really think it's necessary?"

"To tell the truth, I can't really say. There are a lot of crazies in the world, people who are often offended by the messages you deliver in your stories. Not everyone is crazy enough to come after you simply because of your ideals. It may be that the threat died two years ago, but it's got to be your decision," Margo says. "I couldn't possibly advise you on this."

"I've been wondering what it will feel like without someone watching over us. I thought I'd feel more naked, somehow. Maybe I would, if that man hadn't come here to give me a gift from himself and his deceased wife. Somehow, I feel safe and secure. Tressa no longer has nightmares. She's well adjusted and happy, doesn't seem to feel threatened in any way. I think she deserves to grow up without people looking over her shoulders and their own. You suggested that I live and breathe again. Well, last night, for the first time since the attack, I actually did. Things are good."

Margo smiles at him, confident that he is making the right decision. She says, "Now I'm intrigued. So what's her name?"

He looks up. "Her name is Essie Dantzler."

Margo pretends to be surprised. "Your gorgeous neighbor, the woman who's watching Tressa?"

"One and the same," Killian says.

Margo drops the pretense. "So Ethyl has done it after all. Damn, she's good!"

"What? Are you telling me that you knew about her match-making scams?"

Margo blushes. "Well, we put our heads together and sized her up pretty good at your housewarming. But you were a bit slow on the uptake."

"I don't believe this. You people are scandalous."

"Yes, but she was the only one around to carry out the plan. I wasn't actively involved beyond cutting her out of the small herd of single women that showed up without dates. Any of the women that were accompanied would have eagerly dumped their dates if you had just bothered to bat an eye. Your neighbor was different, though. She seemed so alone, as were you. She was beautiful and very sexy. Perfect for you. So tell me, Killy, how does it feel?"

His eyes are devilish sparks for a second. His grin is undeniable, and all he says is, "Good."

"Good? That's it?"

"Really good."

"I want all of the details when we're done. Go on and call the women in your life, and then we'll get back to work. However, if you want to shit-can the rest of the day, I wouldn't bark. I really wouldn't."

Killian shakes his head. He dials the number. "Just give me a minute and I'll be down. Thanks for the talk, Margo."

The relationship between this writer and his literary agent is not typical of the industry; they are genuine friends. They often confide, relying on one another's input. However personal it has become over

the years, the relationship has always remained anchored on profes-
sionalism. Theirs is an affiliation that few aspiring writers will ever
realistically achieve with an agent.

CHAPTER 10

# *Run!*

Killian's call is like dessert before supper for Tressa, who hardly misses Jonathan's strong presence and watchful gaze. All she knows is that he's not feeling well; probably caught her cold.

The fried chicken is crisp and well seasoned. Although Tressa still has a cold, Annabelle Dantzler is pleased that the child consumed the drumstick with such passion. Even so, with all that still looms in the realm of unanswered fates, Tressa's appetite only serves to remind both mother and daughter of Latrell's love for Annabelle's cooking. Like the remnants of their appetites, their smiles vanish without trace in a visual link that saddens in unison.

With the mid-afternoon supper cleared from the table, Tressa sits on the kitchen floor to watch her puppy chomp on the scraps. She strokes Dancer's sleek black coat while humming the song that Ms. Annie hummed as she cooked dinner. The child sniffles, tempted to wipe her nose in her sleeve, as would any kid when no one is looking. She uses some tissue instead.

Essie is standing alone before the bay window. Her thoughts are of Killian and of the passionate night they shared. His attention and tenderness swept her beyond the walls of worry, liberating her by precious hours of a pensive energy's release. It, however, is inevitable that her anxieties over Latrell's fate should return to flood her mind with horrible images. Keeping herself together and entertaining an inquisitive child are difficult tasks, but she manages. However, with all that is right and wrong with the world, Essie Dantzler is about to learn the dismal depths.

Annabelle joins her at the window. For the moment, their eyes are as distant as their thoughts. Standing there like silent sentinels, they resemble women waiting to see if the father and sons would be among the trooping column of conquering heroes, returning home at the end of war. With every passing moment, the outcome looks gloomy and gloomier still.

Essie turns to her mother and hugs her, fighting tears that threaten yet again to flow. This mother can feel her daughter's anguish, sharing it and more. She knows it is time that Essie finally hears the unspoken truth. All of it.

"Come and have a seat, Essie. We need to discuss the hard facts."

"Mom, we don't have to . . ."

Fearing that she will not have the courage to go on, she quickly places her fingers to Essie's lips.

Annabelle takes her by the hand and moves toward the loveseat. The mother and daughter sit facing one another with a terribly foreboding moment of silence wedged between them like a shard of bone between teeth.

The morbid hurt in Annabelle's eyes prompts Essie to ask, "What is it, Mom? I keep getting the feeling that there's something you haven't told me. I've had it since you arrived." She gently squeezes her mother's trembling hands.

Annabelle's averted eyes watered and spilled. She looks to the ceiling and begs, "Oh Lord, please forgive me. I should have told her the truth long ago, but I just couldn't, Lord. My pride has gotten in the way, and I just couldn't hurt one to save the other."

She quivers into miserable tears, shaking her head as she raises her timeworn hands to God and heaven.

"What is it, Mom? What's happened?" Essie asks.

"He just . . . he went bad on us, Essie."

"Who are you talking about?"

"Your brother."

"What do you mean? Has Latrell done this sort of thing before? Even if he has, that doesn't make him bad, just irresponsible and immature," Essie says in her brother's defense. "You know he's a good kid, Mom."

"No, he's not. Not anymore, Essie. It is time you know. No more lies will be told, Lord Jesus."

"But—"

Annabelle places her fingers to her daughter's lips. "Hush now, and let it be said. I'm begging you, because this burden will take me to my grave if I don't talk it out, Essie."

Essie relents, fearing this painful communion because Annabelle seems so resolute.

"I've prayed both night and day for your brother, but all that we have done for that boy has gone by the wayside. I did everything I could, but it was a foolish mistake to think that I could handle it without you."

"What do you mean? Please tell me what's been going on in New York," Essie admonishes.

Annabelle takes a deep breath. "It's drugs, Essie. Latrell experimented with hard drugs and got turned out. He doesn't really care about anything or anyone else."

Essie gasps, shocked by the startling revelation. Whatever her brother may have done, this was unexpected. Despite her resistance, Essie's mind races back to Latrell's abrupt appearance in Myrtle Beach. The sequence of events thereafter, forces acid rain to pour from her eyes. She is an intelligent woman. Though her lips say, "No!" her mind and broken heart declares otherwise.

"Essie, you know all the stuff the doctors would pump into Latrell when he gets really sick. The pain is so bad that they would have to give him drugs like codeine, morphine, and Demerol. Nevertheless, I suppose, this other stuff started at school. He always seemed to need more and more money, but I never thought anything of it, Baby. Several months into his senior year, I found out that he'd already quit school. He should have graduated this summer, but somehow he managed to get his tuition money refunded. When I found out that your brother had spent it all on hookers and dope, it broke my heart, Essie. God, he broke my heart. That boy, Lord, that boy!"

"Mom, no. Please don't tell me . . ."

Annabelle threatens to place her fingers to Essie's lips again.

"No, child, you've got to let me finish this thing, because he used you too. About a month before Latrell came down here, I got him into a program. He seemed to be getting better, talking about going back to school and finishing, no matter what. I really thought he meant it all. I thought that he was getting over it, so I promised that I wouldn't tell you that he'd gotten strung out."

"But he didn't get better, did he . . ."

"No. He had me, the counselor, and Pastor Richland fooled. One night, when I was at church, Latrell left the rehab center. He was so desperate that he leaped from a second story window and came to the house to get his car from the garage. I came home to find the car missing, so I called the police and reported it stolen. The police promised to keep an eye out, but they told me to go ahead and contact the insurance company because they never hold out much hope of finding it in one piece. I didn't want to worry Latrell, so I decided to wait until the next evening to tell him, giving the police a chance to find it. I had a woman's auxiliary meeting scheduled, and I had to leave home very early the next day. As I locked the door, the phone rang, but I had to go because my cab was waiting. I thought it was one of the members calling to check on me, but it was the rehab center. They left a message that I never got. You know, Essie, that was the very first time that the same cab driver has ever picked me up twice. I thought it was a good sign. But as I was headed home, I saw his car."

"Where was he going, Mom?"

Annabelle takes a moment to reflect before telling her. "It wasn't your brother, Essie. The cab driver had his car stolen once, so he called the police for me and we followed the car around that neighborhood until they were caught. Can you imagine how I felt, seeing drug pushers pimping your brother's car around so big and bold like that? They didn't seem to have a care in the world."

"What happened? You got the car back and then what?"

"Just the opposite, Sweetheart. The police couldn't do anything about it. Those boys had a signed title, Essie. Latrell had legally sold them the car for little or nothing. He used to love that car, but he just let them have it after you helped pay it off."

Essie's mind reels, grasping for something positive as if she is drowning in a whirlpool.

"When I got home, I called the rehab center. Your brother had already erased the message they left." Annabelle's eyes wilted. "There was a horrible odor in the house. Latrell had come back when he knew I wouldn't be there. I don't know where he had been for two nights, but he returned on his own. I believe he was getting high at the center, before going AWOL. When I confronted him, he came up with another lie. Latrell told us that he owed a drug dealer a lot of money and they threatened to do me harm. Lord, that boy can lie with the best of them."

Essie relives Latrell's story about the car breaking down on his way to Myrtle Beach. She remembers the call from the garage that would not accept a check for repairs on his nonexistent vehicle.

"I hoped to deal with Latrell's addiction without involving you because you were so well adjusted, finally getting on with your new life. Had I known that he'd come here and take advantage of your trust, I would have told you, Essie. He just disappeared from the center again. I was trying to find him in New York, but he'd already come here. When you called and told me about the car, I should have told you the truth, Sweetheart. Please forgive me, Baby. I just didn't know how." Annabelle weeps the miserable tears of a mother whose child is truly lost.

When Essie embraces her, both women are engulfed in a cloud of despair. Thankfully, Tressa has stayed in the kitchen to play with her best friend.

The telephone rings twice before they notice. Essie's hand shakes as she reaches for the receiver, so she hits the speaker button. Their hearts are shredded by what they hear.

Latrell Dantzler's voice is broken of spirit. His distress is forthcoming when he begs, "Help me, Essie. They're killing me slow." There is a miserable whimper and coughing.

Essie shouts, "Latrell, where are you?"

"Oh thank God," Annabelle stammers before knowing all. She clutches her chest as her blood pressure soars.

Latrell whispers, "If you don't give them what they want, they'll kill me. Please. I can't take it anymore. Mama, is that you? I'm so sick. I hurt so bad."

"Just tell us where you are," Annabelle begs.

The phone is taken away from his lips. The electronically altered voice of the kidnapper is harsh and demanding when he says, "I will kill your brother if you don't give me exactly what I want.

When a thin screwdriver is driven into Latrell's leg just above the left knee, his scream rakes across their souls.

"What are you animals doing to my son?" Annabelle shrieks.

Essie says, "Please don't hurt him anymore. Whatever my brother owes you, I'll pay it. Just stop torturing him. What do you want from us?"

"This isn't about money, Bitch! Before I tell you what I want, I'm going to warn you only once. Your telephones, all of them, have been tapped, and high explosives are planted throughout your entire home. If you attempt to notify the police, you and your brother will die."

"What?" Essie looks about the room, detecting nothing. Her mother reads her thoughts, but she cannot move.

"You will die a horrible death if you choose to defy me, Lady, and your brother can't stand much more of this. Do you understand me?"

Essie shouts, "Yes. What do you want from us? I will do anything. Just don't hurt him!"

During a short pause, Latrell whimpers in the background.

"We want the child, or your brother dies!"

Their hearts froze. On cue, Latrell cries out from a well-placed boot.

"Do you hear me, Woman? Bring me the kid and your brother will go free. He doesn't have much time left. He's cold and suffering from exposure. The clock's ticking."

The telephone is placed before Latrell's lips, where an icy mist accompanies his desperate words.

"Give them what they want, Essie. Please, save me. They promised to let me go. Please!"

Annabelle says, "Oh, my poor baby. Why have you people done this to him? He has Sickle Cell Anemia, for God's sake!"

"Please, Essie, I need you. I'm bleeding. God, I hurt so bad. It's so dark and cold here."

Essie's eyes seek her mom's teary face. Her heart is breaking, shattering like compressed bone, grating against her nature. Her quivering lips are finally forced to say, "I can't, Baby. I just can't do that." Essie bursts into tears, shying away from her mother's pleading eyes.

Latrell begins to scream just as Tressa walks into the room to say, "I don't feel so good, Essie." Essie's hand races for the receiver, sparing the child the details of this distressing call.

Annabelle goes to Tressa just as the voice says to Essie, "You have five minutes to meet my demands. At that time, you'll all die!"

The line is silent, but the connection remains intact.

Essie places the receiver on the loveseat and picks up Tressa. She quietly says to her mother, "We have to get out of the house. We have to get Tressa out of here right now."

"But what about your . . ."

Her mother doesn't have to see the hard look in Essie's eyes to go silent. Her son is already lost, and she cannot expect her daughter to surrender this innocent child. She would have repented the thought had Essie not dragged her by the arm toward the kitchen on her way to the garage.

When they pass the telephone on the kitchen countertop, Annabelle Dantzler reaches for it in reflex. As they move further away from it, her fingers seek to still her whimpering lips.

As the puppy follows, Tressa asks, "What's wrong, Essie? Are we going to see the doctor? I feel really sick."

Essie snatches her purse and Tressa's pink coat from the stool by the door. She has to drag her grieving mother down the steps. "Yes, Tressa, we will go to the doctor in a little while. We have to hurry now, Baby. God, you're burning up!"

The puppy leaps into the car when the door opens.

Moments later, after looking at the car's undercarriage and under the hood, Essie pulls out of the garage. At the end of the driveway, she does not hesitate to race into oncoming traffic.

Annabelle covers Tressa's ears and says, "Where are we going, Essie? That crazy man said that they will be watching the police stations. If we go anywhere near them, they'll kill him."

"I know, Mother. I need time to think."

While holding Tressa Prophet in the back seat, Annabelle felt the child's forehead, testing for an increase in temperature with a mother's instinct and sensitivity. Her abated fever has found resurgence.

Tressa coughs before asking, "Do I have to take more medicine, Ms. Annie? It tastes bad."

Essie's alert eyes search the rearview and side mirrors. She swerves to avoid a collision as she races through a caution light, almost hoping to catch the attention of a police officer.

"Not right now, Baby. We'll see what the doctor has to say first," Annabelle says.

"I want my daddy," Tressa whispers. She is scared, easily picking up on the anxieties of the older women. She has come to trust them both with a child's conviction, but she knows that they are keeping something from her. She fears that something has happened to her father, something to do with the bad men.

The black sedan stays well back, but its driver keeps pace with the Jaguar. Sheriff Barnes calls his brother to say, "Things are going as planned. Make sure you stay out of sight. If she doesn't go to her office, you'll know right away. Just be ready to converge on my signal if she doesn't."

A nervous Anthony Barnes asks, "But what if she drives right past me?"

"If she deviates, then we'll ram her and take the kid. Out!"

Essie's anxious hand searches the contents of her purse for her cell phone, but she remembers it's charging at home. She's disheartened until she thinks of her office. The place is deserted on Sundays, but has a state of the art security system. She could call the police from there.

Moments later, the Jaguar's right-turn signal flashes. Essie slows to enter the parking garage, which is adjacent to her office.

She thinks it best to hide her car.

A white van leaves the parking space in front of the StarDantze Real Estate Agency. Two cars back, it enters the parking structure.

Three vehicles proceed to the ramp of level two. Level one and two are full. The van suddenly veers left, up the off-ramp in the opposite direction.

Essie's tires screech as she hurries for the ramp to level three. She doesn't see the white van going up the ramp in the wrong direction, but notices the black sedan in the mirror. Fear seizes her when she realizes that she may have panicked right into their hands by leaving the safety of her home.

"Essie, slow down. You're scaring the child," Annabelle warns.

"Don't look back, Mom. We're being followed."

"Oh no. What are we going to do?"

"When I hit the next ramp, I'll stop. Jump out with Tressa and hide. When they pass by, take Tressa to the stairs. Don't wait for the elevator. Tell the attendant to call the police from downstairs. Take my spare keys and go to my office. The silent alarm will go off when you fail to punch in the code, but I want you to call the police anyway. I can't stop long, so you'll have to hurry. Can you do it, Mom?"

Annabelle looks down at the sweating child as Essie guns it. They scrape the curved wall of the ramp, causing sparks to fly.

Tressa screams, holding her puppy by the nape of the neck.

"But what about you?"

Wham!

When Essie turns the corner, she slams into the white van that had slid to a stop to block her path. The booming collision echoes through the garage, causing car alarms to blare.

The airbag has done its job, but Essie's jaw is hurting. She snatches a ballpoint pen from the console and drives it into the bag three times to deflate it. Desperately fighting for control of the wheel, she forces the transmission into reverse. The car only moves inches before slamming into the black sedan. They are trapped!

Essie tries to gun it just as Roscoe Barnes opens his door to get out. The sheriff is knocked back into his seat as Essie smokes the tires to the steel belts. The stench of burning rubber fills the world before the wounded Jaguar quits on her.

The sheriff gets out and peers through the gray haze. Meanwhile, Anthony Barnes emerges from the side door of the van with Latrell Dantzler in tow.

Essie's and her mother's hearts freeze when he is dragged from the door. He is bloody and limping, barely able to stand. His hands are bound behind his back. His lips are locked into a painful grimace, and black coils encircle his puffy eyes.

As Annabelle shouts his name, her door flies open and she is snatched from the rear of the car. Anthony Barnes places a gun to Latrell's head and asks, "Do you want him dead or alive, Bitch?"

Tressa screams and crawls out on her side, where Essie scoops her up and tries to retreat.

Roscoe Barnes places a gun to Annabelle's head, but the woman's only concern is for her broken son. Anthony Barnes puts his gun in his belt and uses both hands to send Latrell tumbling down the ramp. He comes to rest in a heap just beyond the black sedan's rear bumper. Though he stops rolling, his world continues to reel.

Essie turns to run, but she's cut off. Stuck between two parked cars, she puts the child down behind her.

When Tressa looks into Anthony's face, she knows who he is. When he approaches, the barking puppy begins to growl. Essie launches her fingernails at his eyes, slashing at a masked face.

She screams, "Run, Tressa! Run!"

Dancer breaks away from the child. Fearing nothing and ready to defend Tressa with his life, Dancer charges into the fray. Tressa calls after him, but he keeps going.

With Dancer biting at the bad man's leg, Tressa is paralyzed by fear, and the world becomes nauseatingly slow and silent. Her eyes bulge and her tiny heart races unchecked. She wants to run but she cannot move simply because she knows who these men are.

"Tressa, go!"

Dancer yelps when Anthony Barnes kicks him across the hood of a parked car.

With car alarms blaring, Roscoe Barnes shoves the frail old woman to the floor and kicks her in the gut for good measure. Time is running out.

Though they wore masks, Anthony's flesh is still vulnerable around the eyes and cheekbones. With his face and throat bleeding from Essie's assault, Anthony Barnes heeds his brother's order to end this.

Without further hesitation, the younger Barnes rams his gloved fist into Essie's stomach. Each time he hammers her face and body, she is rocked by memories of her brutal husband. Finally, she succumbs to the blows that rain from Anthony's vengeful hands.

Essie is dizzy, going down for the last time. Although time is of the essence, Sheriff Barnes watches his brother's brutal display with great pride.

Tressa's paralysis breaks too late. She gets down on her hands and knees to crawl beneath the SUV to the left. Dancer whimpers. She can see him lying on his side, injured. He looks at Tressa, trying to crawl to her, but he's too badly hurt to move.

Tressa screams when Anthony grabs her by the ankle to drag her from under the bumper of the parked vehicle. Stars ignite in her head when she is slapped hard. He tosses the limp child to the floor of the van and shuts the door behind her.

When the van moves away, Essie reaches out, crawling through her own blood. Listening to the screeching tires, smothered by a cloud of suffocating exhaust fumes, she is fading. As her eyes flutter, she whispers, "I'm so sorry, Tressa. Killy, please forgive me. Forgive me."

## CHAPTER II

# Dreaded Truth

*M*argo, whose actual surname is Firestone, races for the stairs. She reaches Killian just as he signs the last autograph. She is about to speak when two very grave-looking men in black trench coats rush into the book store, closing on Killian's position.

They look serious enough to cause Margo's breath to pause. As the two strangers approach, she says, "My God. It's true."

"What?" Killian asks, looking over his shoulder to see that terrified gaze.

"Are you Killian Prophet?" the tall Caucasian asks while reaching into his coat for his credentials.

Killian stands quickly, backing away from the table with his heart skipping beats. "Who are you?" he demands, defensively.

"Sir, I'm Agent Sweeney of the FBI. This is Agent Gains. I'm afraid that we have to ask you to come with us."

Killian is suspicious of their identities. Although he has written about such things, he has never actually seen an authentic FBI badge.

"Why? What's happened? I'm not going anywhere with you until you tell me what this is all about."

Sweeney surveys the room. There are strangers about, listening.

He lowers his voice to say, "I will explain everything, Mr. Prophet, in private."

Margo notices Killian's defensive posture, knowing that they are about to get into it. She blurts out, "It's Tressa, Killian. She has been kidnapped. I just saw it on the news!"

Killian gasps, looking at Margo, almost wishing that she were the type to play such a cruel joke. Agent Sweeney purses his lips and nods to confirm the terrible news.

When Agent Gains takes Killian by the arm, the writer stumbles. He is helped to the car. The agent asks Margo to tend to Killian's affairs while he's transported to his home. She does as she's asked, knowing that they must have been forbidden to discuss this case with anyone other than the girl's father. She promises to join him soon.

As the gray Ford leaves the mall, hordes of news teams come pouring in. Killian remains quiet as the details are explained. His mind reels. His heart sinks. Tressa is gone.

Latrell Dantzler is dying. His mother and sister watch as he is attached to the machine. The technician, knowing their distress, explains that a blood transfer is more involved than a simple transfusion. They have to make an incision in his inner thigh so the large catheter can be inserted. As the machine sucks his dying blood from the femoral vein, oxygenated whole blood is pumped back to the heart.

Essie has a mild concussion, but she refuses to stay in her own bed because she finds herself torn between her brother's critical condition and Killian's eventual return to Myrtle Beach. She has attempted to reach him, certain that she is to blame for Tressa's kidnapping. She longs to be at his side—which is also what she fears most.

Wild horses cannot keep Annabelle Dantzler from Latrell's bedside, even with a fractured rib. She promises to stay in the wheelchair, but she will not be moved again. The sympathetic doctor has a bed brought in for her.

Because her son could be dying, Annabelle has to make sure that he repents his sins. Only then will she be satisfied.

Before leaving the hospital against her doctor's wishes, Essie looks down at her mother as she caresses Latrell's bearded face. Annabelle is urging him on, begging him to fight for his life. As she prays with tears flowing from her eyes to the corners of her lips, she looks so old to Essie. Her mother's smooth brown skin seems so dry. Her salt-and-pepper hair reflects no light; its oily luster has disappeared like Latrell's consciousness.

With her head shouting messages of pain, Essie endures the slight dizziness as she reaches for the telephone. She has to call a cab. After kissing Latrell's hot cheeks and hugging her mother, she leaves the hospital, without having any rest.

Before she committed to leaving, Essie Dantzler was given a thorough examination and x-rayed from head to toe. After being questioned repeatedly by the local authorities, the FBI agents took her statement again. Still, she had to go.

The farther away from the hospital she gets and the closer to home she gets, the more her head pounds.

Although South Carolina's Governor Sanders has never met the author, he lights a fire under the FBI at the urging of his wife. Over a dozen field agents have been dispatched to bring this sad episode to an end.

Special Agent in Charge Anjon Lee, considered one of the FBI's best hostage negotiators, has flown in from Quantico, Virginia. Close on his heels is Special Agent Angela Siegle, who directs the setup of the communications post as she prepares to trace the whereabouts of the kidnappers when they finally decide to make contact.

Siegle is a young black woman with drive and determination, hoping to head her own kidnapping investigation team someday. For the time being, however, she is content to learn all that one of the very best has to offer.

During the last five years of their alliance, Anjon Lee and Angela Siegle have solved over a dozen such cases, with the safe return of eleven abduction victims in the mid-Atlantic region alone. Their contrasting styles and angles of attack seem less a hindrance than a compliment to their discerning assistant director, who often refers to them as his A-team. Special Agent Lee, a Japanese-American, is the psychoanalytical genius of the two. He maintains that getting into the kidnapper's head is usually the most progressive means of investigation. It is Agent Lee's belief that a criminal's motivation to commit his crimes, more often than not, leads to his capture.

Ms. Siegle is more the forensic and technological wizard. She is a profiler with a command of the FBI database and the web. They were partnered nearly six years ago, after Lee's former partner suffered a mental breakdown upon becoming emotionally involved in a particularly tragic case. In many ways, that changing of the guards has been evolutionary. It was simply the survival of the fittest.

Anders and Ethyl Prophet arrive several hours after Killian's return. Like so many cases past and future, an investigating police officer kept his promise to a friend in the media. For that reason, the child's grandparents learned of the kidnapping from the television. The reporter who got the scoop gained the favor of executives, despite the very painful consequences for a family that was yet to be contacted by authorities. Such, unfortunately, is life.

Two of the agents assigned to the case are relegated to patrolling the perimeter of Killian Prophet's estate. They will keep an eye out for anything or anyone that seems out of place, while keeping roving reporters at bay. Because the media compromised the investigation so quickly, the local police cannot be trusted to keep their mouths shut.

Other investigators are dispatched to the scene of the kidnapping and to the local precinct to gather any additional physical evidence, if any. One remains at the hospital in case Latrell Dantzler regains consciousness, but they figure that if he could offer anything of use concerning the whereabouts or identities of the kidnappers, he would not be alive.

Killian's worried parents are attempting to comfort him in the family room while Agent Lee familiarizes himself with this case. Killian has been briefed on how to deal with the kidnappers when they call, warned against being confrontational. He was advised to agree to their demands, coached on how to keep them talking.

As Lee goes over the scant case file in the day room, Angela Siegle takes a call from Detective Marlowe of Myrtle Beach Metro. She pokes her head in to say, "They found the van. Are you coming?"

Agent Lee picks up another, more heavily documented case file. "No. You go ahead," he says without looking up. "I trust your instincts, Angela. Let's hope the locals haven't contaminated the scene. Call me if you find anything, but I doubt that you will."

While looking over the case file of the Wilmington Beach assassination attempt, he winces when he sees the position of Miranda Prophet's body.

Agent Siegle asks, "What prompts you to say that?"

He turns around, peering over the rim of his glasses to say, "You know why. These men are extremely organized. They actually committed the first kidnapping to instigate the second.

I seriously doubt they'd leave a vehicle that can lead us to them, but we must process all the evidence."

Agent Siegle leaves without another word, knowing that he is probably right. About two blocks away, her phone rings. "One more thing, Angela," Lee says. "Put Davis on the female reporter that broke the story, the one at the parking garage with the good contacts. Because she left so suddenly, I suspect that she'll show up at the site of the abandoned abduction vehicle. I want her watched, just in case her contact violates us again. Tell Davis to be discrete."

Approximately eight hours have already passed without a call. The kidnappers should have made their demands known by now, but they seem to be in no hurry to make contact. With the passing hours, Killian Prophet recedes further into himself. While rocking back and forth near the telephone, he ravages his fingernails.

Ethyl Prophet's nerves are so frazzled that her only recourse is to cook dinner. She sees to it that the agents have gotten something to eat, although she is surprised that they eat her cooking. She thinks that they must be forbidden to accept food from victims. She insists that they cannot think on empty stomachs, and it is a sin to waste good food.

All of the drapes are drawn in the home to deny prying eyes. When Agent Richards opens the door to allow the disheveled and severely bruised Essie Dantzler entrance, she holds herself as if the room is cold. At first, her eyes cannot meet those of Ethyl Prophet. She also fears the grandmother's initial reaction to her, what she might feel. Nevertheless, her many uncertainties are soon answered.

Ethyl looks into her eyes with great compassion. When Killian's mother reaches for her battered face, Essie flinches. Ethyl could not leave her all alone, out there in a world so full of pain. When Essie Dantzler finally looks Tressa's persistent grandmother in the eyes, they share a sadness that needs no verbalization. Fearing that she will shy away, Ethyl closes the gap and embraces her. As she holds her son's neighbor and friend, both women begin to weep.

With her head upon Ethyl's shoulders, Essie says, "I'm so sorry, Ethyl. They tricked me into running." With a voice reflecting misery and grief, Essie is not unlike a child herself. "I tried to stop them. I tried so hard."

"I know, Child. Just let it all out. Hush now. Shhhh."

Moments later, they sit together. After spending much of this time in silence, Essie says, "They questioned me over and over again, as if they thought that I was involved. Why did they have to treat me that way?"

Ethyl is sympathetic and hates what she is about to say, but feels it best. "They were just doing their job, Sweetheart. You did get your brother back, after all."

Essie is shocked by what sounds like another accusation, even from Ethyl's lips. "What?" Her eyes burn and her saliva turns to bile. She winces, as if a fist comes at her again.

It is too profound to miss. Ethyl touches her shoulder with great care and asks, "Are you okay, Essie?"

Essie backs away from her touch while experiencing painfully vivid images that exist for her horrified eyes only. Then she places her face in her palms.

"And Killian . . . what does he think?" Essie asks, hoping to hear something positive in his mother's voice.

Ethyl looks away. She sighs, finally saying, "He's worried sick. I don't know what Killy is thinking right now because he is shutting everyone out. When the authorities aren't questioning him about enemies and such, he just sits by the phone. He won't talk. He won't eat. I think he just went upstairs before you came in."

"I shouldn't be here. I know it."

"Nonsense. You should see him, but I should talk to him first," Ethyl suggests.

Essie's hands tremble in the wake of another brutal flashback. Her entire body seems to be a ball of mini-tremors. She whispers, "I'm so afraid. He hates me, doesn't he?"

Ethyl squeezes her hand. "I'll let Killian know that you're here. Please promise me that you won't leave without speaking to him first. He really needs us all right now. I believe my son blames himself because he thinks that his writing has brought all this pain down on the people he loves. That kind of guilt is dangerous. Please, promise that you won't leave."

Essie Dantzler promises to stay, but she isn't sure that she will keep it.

Anders is in Killian's bedroom, trying to get his distraught son to open up. He is reminded of Killian's stay in the mental institution. It is very unsettling to see his son so withdrawn, not knowing if he is slipping toward that dark abyss once again. The silence is deafening.

Anders is relieved when his wife comes in. She always seems better equipped to deal with such things. In truth, Ethyl can only rely on her faith in God to protect her grandchild. In this case, however, she needs a mother's instincts to deal with her son's depression, not quite sure if she is about to do the right thing.

Anders moves toward the bedroom door to whisper, "Anything new?"

She whispers, "The police and FBI are doing everything they can, but nothing so far. How is he?"

"Just staring out the window. He's been standing there for the last thirty minutes and still won't talk to me. Have you heard anything about his friend?"

"Essie is downstairs. That poor girl is barely recognizable right now. She must have put up one hell of a fight. She's really afraid to face Killian right now, but I think it best that she does."

Anders whispers, "Do you really think that's wise? I know the authorities have put her through the wringer, but a confrontation between them now might get messy."

Ethyl knows her husband's words have merit, but she is relying on intuition. Her son could not leave the house to visit the hospital while awaiting the call that never came. He could have called to check on her, but he did not. Given his state of mind, Ethyl is beginning to think that to be a good thing because he needs to see Essie in this wretched state. He needs to accept that fact that Essie is also a victim. She hopes that Killian remembers that he loves this woman.

"I know that this may cause more harm than good, but they spent their first night together just last night. Tressa called and told me. It must have meant something more to Killian than sex. I believe they are in love, and we have to give that love a chance. Only the Lord knows how this is going to turn, but turn it must, Andy."

"You've been meddling, and now you have our grandchild issuing regular reports," her husband says with a hint of disgust.

"Now is not the time," Ethyl says. She moves toward her son at the far end of the bedroom where he stares into nothingness.

Anders watches from afar. He knows that it is not going well when Killian places a hand in the air with his fingers splayed to halt his mother's words. She is pleading with him, that much is obvious.

Sudden movement causes Anders to look over his shoulder just in time to see Essie's sad eyes turn away. After a dreadfully lonely walk up those steps, what Essie has just seen is confirmation that the man she loves has found a way to hate her.

Anders's heart goes out to the woman. As Essie turns to walk away, he gently takes her by the arm and hugs her. He leads her into the room where she and Killian made love the night before.

As they cross the room, Anders prays that his wife is right about them.

Anders and Essie stop midway and Ethyl takes her by the hand, urging her forth. Essie is reluctant to face Killian. The closer she gets to him, the more that furious pain in her head seems to rage. Staring at Killian's back with a longing to touch him, she stops shy of her lover because he seems so rigid.

Ethyl urges her on. She looks up at her son and says softly, "To err is human, Son, and to forgive is of a divinity that we all must face some sweet day. Would you rather that both the women in your life be lost to the same tragic moment? This is not her fault, Killian. She loves Tressa and she fought for that child. I believe that she fought hard—even at the risk of her own life."

Ethyl takes Killian's right hand and Essie's left, placing them together. She coerces Essie to stand before him and walks away.

When Killian finally looks at Essie, his eyes water. His hurt for her and his child makes itself known, as a tidal wave will leave its mark upon the shore. This is the first time Killian has seen Essie since leaving Tressa in her care. It is the first time that he sees Essie's swollen lips and jaw, and black eye. All of his anger and rage are defused. His heart and arms go out to her.

They embrace, sobbing in one another's arms. Ethyl holds her husband's hand, thanking God for some resolution. Then they leave them alone, shutting the door to give them privacy.

Once they have talked a bit, Ethyl goes to Essie's house and gathers some of her things. When Ethyl returns, she gets Essie cleaned up and convinces her to lie down in a quiet room. Ethyl will never know the terrible nightmares Essie Dantzler faces in her restless dreams, but Killian senses each blow as he watches over her.

Agent Siegle returns at midnight with bad news. It is no surprise to find Agent Lee sitting at the table, delving deeper into the morbid details of the old case file.

Without ceremony, she says, "The van that crashed through the tollgate of the parking garage was found about three blocks from there, which leads me to believe that the abduction site was no coincidence. The vehicle was torched to destroy evidence."

"Registration?"

"We recovered the VIN number." Siegle checks her notes and looks at a map of the region. "The van is registered to a Janis Pearls. It was used for deliveries in Sumter, South Carolina. She reported it stolen a little over three weeks ago. Once they had the girl, they exchanged vehicles right away to evade the local police. We were able to find two different blood types from the outer door handles, one of which matches that of Latrell Dantzler. The other blood type is B-positive, matching the sample taken from Ms. Dantzler's fingernails."

"And the other car?" Lee asks.

"The abandoned vehicle in the parking garage was stolen over four weeks ago from Columbia, South Carolina. They were plotting this thing for weeks, maybe even longer."

"These men are professionals. They had nearly all the angles covered. One of them could be Miranda Prophet's killer, the one that got away. Tactics suggest that they watched the writer's family for quite some time before making their move. They just didn't count on the child's new puppy, nor that the writer might not stay put after the bedroom lights went out. He went downstairs to work on his latest project, where he fell asleep at his desk. He was awakened by his daughter's screams after the puppy sounded the alarm. Apparently the alarm system was circumvented."

"Motive seems obvious enough," Siegle added.

"Even though Mr. Prophet's work was fictional, they hated his goals and ideals so much that they decided to murder him up close and personal. No high-powered rifle would do for them. They wanted to enjoy it first. On a wall, one of them used a magic marker to scrawl the words, 'Let's see you write about this in hell, nigger.' These men probably meant to torture the family before killing them all. No matter how much physical pain his family would be made to suffer, it would have been infinitely more painful for Prophet to watch."

"Maybe Klan or some other hate group," Agent Siegle suggests.

"More probable than not. They may be affiliated, but I don't count on brazen participation. I believe that career orientations and the dedication with which these men executed their plans may force them to conceal their hatred of blacks," Agent Lee speculates.

"Every time a Klansman is accused of a crime, he's always referred to as a former member of the KKK," Siegle says. "Who are we looking for? Their tactics are almost flawless, and they have access to voice altering technology. Who?"

"Law enforcement, disgruntled or retired perhaps," Lee says bluntly. He gauges Angela's reaction because a crooked cop murdered her father years ago, and he wants to make sure that she has moved on.

"We managed to lift two boot prints from the scene of the torched van. Preliminary reports show that they are standard government issue—the same type found at the scene two years ago."

"Makes sense that they're disgruntled cops, since they've neglected to ask for a ransom thus far. This case bothers me because it may never have been about money. Somehow it's always been very personal to these guys."

Despite Angela's fears that this one will be a tragic loss for all concerned, she pushes her focus to the challenges ahead because personal feelings are inherent dangers on the job. As with life's many lessons of joy and pain, all things seem to share connections.

"I will believe in good, because it's our duty to define the discerning difference from evil," Siegle says aloud to no one other than herself.

"What other theories have you devised, Angela?"

"It's pretty obvious to me that they planned the attack on the bodyguards' parents to draw them away. The brothers are reputed protectors. Each has taken a bullet for a client, never having lost one. They were a near perfect fit, and I applaud Mr. Prophet's choice in bodyguards. In fact, the only flaw I can find is that they are kin. It left the kidnappers a small window, not actually knowing whether Mr. Prophet would immediately commission new watchers. Their timing was succinct. The bodyguards' father is murdered with great skill while his wife sleeps. He stabs her as she tries to run, but does not kill her. The intruder pulls the knife from her shoulder and drives it into her leg. He does not stab her in the chest or back, even though he is clearly standing over her body at the time."

Agent Lee says, "That's why I believe we're looking for at least three men, possibly four. They gambled on the neighbor running with the child. There is only one way off this street and out of this neighborhood. The threat of explosives was an ingenious ploy to flush Ms. Dantzler out of her comfort zone. With her brother's tortured screams in the background, she didn't really have time to think."

Siegle agrees and says, "I'm told her alarm system is comparable to this one. That's why they didn't risk it. But as determined as they seemed to be, I'm almost certain that they would have planned an alternative escape from this peninsula because they would have broken in."

"They wouldn't have left any witnesses if that was the case because they already studied the protocol of the resident security. Their biggest worry was probably the response time of the local police, but they would have come in, if she'd stayed put. I checked, and there have been three false reports of domestic violence in the area made at exactly the same time of day. All three calls were made from stolen cell phones. This alone holds profound implications."

Agent Lee's phone rings. He answers it, scribbles down some notes, and hangs up.

"The nanny claims to have been threatened, so she left here without warning Mr. Prophet of the potential danger."

"Hmm. Given the nature of Prophet's relationship with his neighbor, the kidnappers figured that he would leave the child with her, rather than cancel the promotion of his new book. Damn! If she had only said something, this may have been avoided," Siegle says.

"Ms. Borja was a nervous wreck when Simons showed up to question her. She blurted it all out before he could initiate the interview. I believe she's clean, but we'll do a deeper background check, just in case there's more to it."

"Imagine how differently things might have been if she had just told that man the truth. Mr. Prophet would have battened down the hatches had he known. I bet she never works as a nanny again. Not around here," Agent Siegle says with antipathy. She scowls, thinking of the nanny's possible complicity in this matter. The remote possibility almost seems more palatable than the fact that Ms. Borja was just a cowardly victim.

"These men are good. They've developed a very keen insight into human behavior," Lee says as he reaches for a neglected cup of tea.

Siegle sits at the table to consult her laptop. Moments later she says, "Think of the time and energy they must have expended on their individual homework assignments. Video feeds from different traffic cams show that the sedan was following Ms. Dantzler all the way. Another traffic cam proves that the van joined the chase from the opposite direction, traveling south on Lister Avenue toward her real estate office and the parking garage. Facial features were obscured by ski masks. This trap was sprung the moment she left home."

"What's Mr. Prophet's net worth, Angela?"

A moment later she says, "Just under ten point two million, not including this property. But neither of us believes this to be about money, so why did you ask?"

Lee says, "I'm hoping that one of them finds out and gets greedy. Maybe we should make it public knowledge. Even so, it's still wishful thinking on my part."

"And?"

"And I fear that we're going to have to keep a watchful eye on Killian Prophet. They really want him. Think about this for a moment. Why didn't they attack him at the book signing when he became vulnerable? Why would they go through all of this trouble when they could have gone directly to the source of their disdain?"

She thinks about it for a second. "The mall was crowded and extra security would have been assigned. By snatching the child, they derive some pleasure in knowing that Prophet would be distraught. This may be an oversimplification, but I believe that torture is a tool they want to use against him because something in Prophet's writing has offended them in some way."

Agent Lee puts away the photos. He smiles and says, "Very astute of you, Agent Siegle. Have the data sent from the Sumter and Columbia areas where the transport vehicles were stolen."

Angela Siegle observes silently as Agent Lee stands before the board to draw a nearly perfect circle around Columbia, Sumter, and Myrtle Beach. He says, "I have a sneaking suspicion that these kidnappers are even closer than that. I don't have enough to put it together, but I'm almost certain that Mr. Prophet has built his new home right in the devil's backyard.

"One of your feelings, Mr. Lee?"

"One of my feelings, Agent Siegle." He sighs.

She picks up the phone and requests the data on the thefts. As she does so, rain begins to fall. The temperature is dropping, and early December snow is in the forecast.

## CHAPTER 12

# The Barn

The barn is cold and quiet, except for the frigid wind that whistles through the cracks. Hay covers the floor of Tressa's cage. She is freezing and alone, terrified that she'll never see her father again. Her mind replays the images of her capture and of Essie's futile attempt to defend her. Her soul mate, Dancer, cursed by name from her own lips, is hurt.

Tressa is coughing much more than before, and she is sweating profusely. The child, having long abandoned her cries for help, lies curled in the fetal position on a bed of musty straw under a moth-eaten blanket. Her nose refuses to stop running, so she has to wipe it on a sleeve of the pink coat, which now offers inadequate warmth.

An opossum scurries into the barn before catching her alien scent. It is returning from a night of scavenging when it smells the child in its abode. It hisses when it sees her staring eyes. Before moving on, it bares its teeth for good measure, but the child does not react in fear. She does not react at all.

When Tressa finally coughs, the animal breaks its gaze and scampers through a hole in a wall. Its long white tail seems to take an eternity to disappear.

Rain begins to fall, banging like hail on the rusted tin roof overhead. Tressa shivers, closing her eyes to pray like her mother and grandmother have taught her to do in good times and bad. Tressa Prophet's first dawn in hell is on the horizon.

Annabelle Dantzler sobs at her son's bedside. She too prays, because the doctors have done everything they can for Latrell, but his bodily systems have been weakened considerably by his drug abuse and anemia. After two weeks of malnutrition, torture, and exposure to fluctuating temperatures, his will to fight is failing. If Latrell doesn't begin to recover soon, he is doomed.

Annabelle cannot leave his side. Even after all of the lies and deception, he still does not deserve to die alone. Such is a mother's love, buried to the core of her aching bones.

Two days have passed without word from the kidnappers, and Killian has become irritable. He is restless and understandably pensive. His feeling of helplessness is unbearable.

The FBI agents assigned to this case have been frustrated at every avenue of investigation, running into one dead end after another. The first twenty-four hours is considered the most effective period for gathering useful evidence. In this case, however, the kidnappers' motives are unsubstantiated. There has been no ransom demand, leading most to believe that this crime is motivated by other than financial gain. Hatred and vengeance are openly considered. Unfortunately, Tressa's life is on the line.

Margo First is calling from 10,000 feet. When the phone starts to ring, everyone scrambles to his or her post.

Agent Siegle oversees the trace, keeping Killian at bay until the fourth ring. All are soon disheartened to hear Margo's voice. Every time something like this happens, everyone inside the Prophet home is greatly disappointed.

"Killian? Hi. I'll be landing soon and coming over, if that's okay. Has there been any word?"

Killian holds his face in his hand, fighting to restrain himself. He whimpers miserably for a second before reining himself in to whisper, "It's okay, Margo. No news yet. We thought this call might finally be them."

"Oh, I'm so sorry. I just felt so awful because I didn't come and offer my support right away," she says.

"Don't worry about it. I have room here if you would like to stay. You're always welcome."

"Thanks. I'll take you up on your offer." There is a pause.

"Killy?"

"Yes?"

"She's going to be all right. Don't ask me how I know, but I do. Just keep the faith."

"Thanks. We'd better clear the lines now. I'll see you when you arrive." He hangs up and stares at the phone.

Having neglected to turn it off, Margo's cell phone chimes once just as the seatbelt sign comes on. Upon reading the text message, she shudders and nearly drops it to the floor. The terrified woman looks around first-class as if the devil himself could be flying the friendly skies with her. She takes a Valium—just one, to calm her nerves.

Agents Siegle and Lee are contemplating the map. They are looking at the Wilmington, North Carolina, area, seeing no commonalities with Myrtle Beach, South Carolina, other than that both homes are in a beach town.

The white tacks planted in Wilmington Beach and Charlotte represent the crime scene of two years ago and the hometown of the two men Killian Prophet killed during the first attack. Black tacks represent the cities from which the vehicles were stolen. A red one represents North Myrtle Beach, where men described as police snatched Latrell Dantzler. There is a blue tack in the Chesapeake Bay area, where the bodyguards' elderly parents were attacked. Finally, Tressa Prophet's abduction is indicated.

Overlapping circles represent the cases that are somehow linked. Of course, the kidnappers could have left the country by now. However, Agent Lee is convinced that they could be within a 200-mile radius. The red, white, and black pinpoints are very important facets of his theory. He is operating on a gut feeling, pleased that Agent Siegle seems to agree.

She draws a larger circle to encompass both areas and says, "I just know they're in here, somewhere. But where exactly?"

"That's the million-dollar question. I think it's time we put your computer skills to the test once again, Agent Siegle. Look for any anomalies within the relative time index of the Wilmington attack. There's really not much else we can do. No sense in both of us being bored."

She looks at the map and then at Killian in the other room.

"Still think they're cops?" she asks.

"Don't you?"

"More and more," she replies. "This is a very frustrating case. We seem to have less than nothing to go on. DNA registry is required now of all law enforcement personnel for their own good, and that of public safety. Nevertheless, it's not perfect. Some townships have been known to deliberately slip people through the cracks because of criminal histories or for insurance purposes, especially in the less sophisticated precincts. Sometimes, unfortunately for people like us, it turns out to be more purposeful than accident. It leaves us so damn little to work with."

Lee looks over his glasses at her. "We have Prophet, and he's what they want. It's just a matter of time before they make a move."

"If they don't, it'll probably mean the girl's already dead."

"That would be tragic. It may just destroy him. We don't want that on our conscience or records, now do we?"

"Hell no."

Margo is given entrance, although Agent Lee has asked that uninvolved well-wishers be kept to a minimum. Ethyl Prophet is her first familiar face. They'd gotten to know each other quite well during Killian's mental breakdown and breakthroughs.

Margo is greeted with the customary embrace and a peck on the cheek, but Ethyl notices a slight difference in her son's agent. She simply attributes it to the oppressive atmosphere.

Anders greets her next. It is a somber occasion, unlike the jovial times of the recent past, when all was well. He attributes her immediate need to speak to Killian to friendly concern.

If nothing else, Margo First is very professional. Keeping her emotions in check has always benefited her career as a literary agent. She knows how to keep her cool, usually making it a point not to become too involved in the private affairs of her clients. Killian, however, has always been different.

Even with a Valium anchor, Margo is scared stiff, holding it all inside because of the monstrous role that is suddenly thrust upon her.

Killian is sitting alone, looking through the thin curtains of the sliding glass door. She approaches him only when certain that they will be left alone. He seems unaware of Margo's presence until she intrudes upon the silence.

"Hey. How are you?"

Killian's eyes are murky and distant when he finally meets her gaze. His response is, "Hey, yourself. I'm alive, but I'm afraid that's the long and short of it."

Killian rises to embrace her, unsure if it is for her benefit or his own. As they hug, Margo peers over his shoulder. His observant father is watching from the other room.

"Killian, listen—we have to talk in private, right now. It is very important that we be discrete."

"I don't feel much like talking right now."

"It's about Tressa. Please do as I ask."

He tries to take a step back. His reaction prompts Margo to hold him fast because they're still being watched.

He asks in a whisper, "What is it?"

"Not here, Killian."

She releases him after the long hug and they move into a corner of the room. Once out of sight, she reaches into her bra for an envelope. It is unopened, but not for long.

"I received this cryptic text message, which directed me to a certain payphone downtown. I found this envelope taped beneath it. They must have figured that I was here, since we were together when you got the news. It's a good thing I was on my way."

"They want me to trade myself for her," he whispers. "If the authorities become involved in any way, they'll kill her without hesitation."

"Oh no," Margo gasps, as he continues to read silently. "Killian, I'm not sure that I did the right thing. God, this is bad. This is very bad. You have to tell them."

Killian holds her tight for a moment, looking into her eyes. "You couldn't do otherwise without costing Tressa her life. Look at what they've already done just to get to me. These people aren't fucking around here."

He looks at the Polaroid photo of his daughter, sharing this angry and hopeful moment with Margo. Tressa is blindfolded, captured by a sea of black and nothing more. "At least we know she's alive," he whispers. "She's alive."

"But what are you going to do? Even if those people keep their word by letting her go, they're going to kill you for sure." Margo searches his eyes for some other solution.

He takes her Blackberry and deletes the message. Once he removes the battery, he gives it back. "I have no choice. That's why you're going to keep it to yourself. I don't care what happens to me, as long as Tressa's safe."

"How will you get out of here? They're watching you like a hawk, and it's probably because they know the asking price."

"Don't worry," he says. "Before this house was completed, I added escape passages from all the bedrooms, in case of another home invasion, or maybe a fire. I can get out, but you have to promise not to say anything."

"Can I help in any way?"

"No. You've done enough for us, Margo. Thank you. Please don't say anything. Promise me this one thing. Swear it to me!"

She nods and kisses him on the cheek. While she sheds tears, they embrace for what is surely the last time. When she wipes her tears away, Margo notices Anders watchful gaze from the doorway.

Anders had not meant to be seen, but he heard nothing of the conversation. He enters the room and asks, "Son, is everything all right?"

"I'm fine, Dad. I think I'll lie down for a while. I'm exhausted."

"You do that, Son. I'll see that Margo is taken care of." Anders joins them. "Your mother and I are planning to go next door to check on Essie in a little while."

Killian's heart skips a beat. "No. No, don't do that, Dad. I'll call her when I get upstairs. She's supposed to be going to the hospital soon."

Anders looks at him, noting a change in his demeanor. Ethyl comes in to invite Margo to eat something. She agrees, but she doesn't really have the appetite to eat much.

The desperate father goes directly to his bedroom and locks the door. He rifles the junk drawer of the dresser, the one everyone has. There, he locates a razor knife and draws its blade to its length. He goes into his closet to grab an old pair of high-tops.

After removing the lace from one shoe, Killian pulls the tongue out of the way to get to the padding. Then he uses the razor to carve out a space in the inner sole.

When someone suddenly knocks on his bedroom door, the blade slips and slashes his left index finger. He yelps as the pain stings him from within the shoe.

"Who is it?" he growls impatiently.

"It's me, Son. Open up. I have some news."

Killian tosses a towel on the bed to cover his things before going to see what his father has found out. The moment he unlocks the door, Anders barges in.

Noticing the bloody finger, he asks, "What's happened?"

"Nothing," Killian lies. "What have you heard, Dad?"

"I lied because I knew you wouldn't unlock the door."

Killian grunts and returns to the bed, anxious to resume his work.

"Well, are you going to tell me what Margo said, or am I going to have to guess?"

Killian looks at his father spitefully. "What? How did you know?"

"I'm an attorney, remember? I can smell a bail-jumper from a mile away," Anders says. He snatches the towel from the bed, revealing the razor and the gutted shoe. His father picks up a wad of rubber and looks at the bloody razor. "What the hell are you up to?"

Killian places his hand over his father's lips. "Shhhh! You have to be quiet about this, or Tressa is dead. They want to make a trade—me for her."

"What? Are you insane? They'll murder you both."

"Keep your voice down!" Killian demands with a growl. "She's my child. I've lived a lot longer than Tressa, and she deserves any chance I can give her. I've got no choice and you know it."

Anders retreats to shut the bedroom door. His heart thuds when he turns around and sees that his son has disappeared. Sweat begins to steam from his forehead.

Killian emerges from the walk-in closet with a mahogany box, which Anders recognizes because he gave it to Killian as a gift years ago.

Killian looks at his father and sits on the bed to pull the last piece of rubber from the sole of the sneaker. Anders stands there, scratching the short hairs of his head for a moment. A long sigh finally escapes his lips before he goes to the bathroom to get a bandage for Killian's finger.

Reluctantly, Killian allows his father to administer first aid. When his finger no longer bleeds, he opens the mahogany box and removes the nickel-plated derringer. He loads the small gun with two .22 caliber longs and slides the over-and-under weapon into the slot prepared for it. He restrings the lace and puts on the sneaker, drawing it tight to make sure it wouldn't come off. It is very uncomfortable, causing him to limp slightly.

"I know what you're thinking, but they'll come looking for us sooner if we're both missing in action. I need you to stay here and pretend that nothing's changed," Killian says.

"But, Son . . ."

As he faces his father, Killian slowly fills his lungs and exhales a deep sigh, then says, "Dad, you told me once that it's not what we've gained in life, but what we're willing to sacrifice that defines the true measure of a man. Please, Dad. Please."

Anders is silent, rising from the bed as his son throws on a heavy leather jacket. He weeps when he embraces Killian, knowing that he'll never see his son alive again, and that Ethyl will hate him for this conspiracy of silence.

Killian kneels to pet Dancer, who's stayed in his room since the veterinarian placed a plaster cast on his front leg.

The puppy lays on the carpet with a broken leg, listless and unhappy. "Don't worry, Boy. I'll send her home to you if I can't deliver her personally." The puppy whimpers. "Hush now. Don't you fret, because it wasn't your fault. I want you to grow up big and strong so you can protect her from all harm." Dancer barks once and licks his hand.

Killian moves toward the closet with his father close on his heels. "She'll be coming back, even if I won't. I want you and mom to help Essie to raise my daughter. Please see to it that Tressa and Essie stay in touch. Promise me that, Dad. I love you."

"I promise, Son. I promise you that Essie will always be a part of Tressa's life," Anders says in tears. "Please God, bring them both home safely."

Killian enters the closet and forces his suits to the left to reveal a hidden door. There are five electronically activated lights on a panel to the right of the door, each an indicator for the other passages. If there were ever another attack, or a fire that kept him from reaching his daughter, he would know if she used the secret passageway to escape, because the first light would come on.

Killian looks at his father one last time to say, "Don't let Mom hold this against Margo, because she only did what she had to. Tell the old lady that I love her."

Killian slides the door open and disappears. Moments later, he emerges downstairs on a carpet of snow on the north side of the house, facing the vine-covered wall between his home and Essie Dantzler's property. When he is sure that no one is watching, Killian streaks toward the wall and opens the wrought iron gate, slipping into his neighbor's yard unnoticed.

Anders is still upstairs in the bedroom, praying for divine intervention while looking down at Killian's footprints in the newly fallen snow.

The writer is about to cross the driveway when he looks at the road and freezes. Across the street, amid snow flurries, two FBI agents are checking out a van that has been parked there all day.

With his back pressed against a wall, Killian sidesteps toward the beach. He ducks behind a column of Essie's house, then leaps the patio railing into the backyard a moment later. He prays that she's still home, counting the seconds until her bruised face appears between the curtains.

Essie unlocks the door and he enters quickly. Killian is out of breath and nervous. Fearing the worst, she asks what happened.

"She's alive, Essie. Tressa is alive,"

She hugs him, wincing from her bruises. "Oh, thank God!"

"They're willing to release my daughter, but only if I agree to trade myself for her freedom."

"What?" she says with a grimace. Tears immediately begin to fill her eyes because she knows what he means to do. "No. No, Killy."

"I need your help, Essie. I have to get away without the FBI's knowledge. I'll need your wagon. Will you help me?"

"But they'll kill you," she says, backing away. "They'll kill you sure as shit, Killian. You can't go!"

Killian takes her arms firmly in her grasp and looks directly into her fearful eyes to say, "Time is running out. I'm begging you. If I fail to rendezvous with them in a matter of hours, Tressa will die. She needs to go to a hospital right away. Don't you see? My life is meaningless if my daughter dies in my place. You must help me."

"But I'll never see you again," she whimpers. "I love you, Killy. I love you so much." Essie sobs miserably.

"And I love you, but we're not the issue here—Tressa is. Will you lend me the car?"

She wipes her tears. "No," she says.

He backs away with fire in his eyes. "How can you say that to me?"

"I'm coming with you," she says.

"You can't."

She stares back at him resolutely. "How else will you be sure that Tressa reaches safety? You can't just call up a taxi and tell the driver to make sure that your kidnapped daughter gets home. We're in this together, Killian, or not at all."

Killian cannot refute her logic, because he hasn't thought this all the way through. Although it places Essie in harm's way, he agrees.

Moments later Essie's Volvo wagon lurches onto the snowy streets of South Myrtle Beach with Killian Prophet sitting on the floor. It's slow going until they cross the Highway 17 Bypass, heading northwest on the 501.

Wrapped in nail-biting silence, knowing something of impending doom, they drive westward. Highway 378 takes them toward Conway, South Carolina, and Killian Prophet's ugly destiny.

## CHAPTER 13

# *To the Letter*

At 3:33 p.m., Essie Dantzler's answering machine kicks in. After the beep, there is a moment of mournful weeping.

Cracked and drained of life, her mother's voice announces that her brother is in the hands of God. There is a clatter when the receiver hits the floor and sounds of rushing footsteps. Concerned voices soon fill the air. Annabelle Dantzler is overwhelmed by the sorrow of watching her son's slow death. Her only solace is that Latrell regained consciousness long enough to repent his sins. With her guidance, Latrell Dantzler asked God to forgive his wretched soul.

*Tressa is in peril! Killian is alone in a dreary swamp, running down a path that winds through Douglas-fir and cedar trees whose limbs are*

*matted and laden with snow. Except for the sound of his crunching footsteps and a low murmur that comes and goes with an ominous breeze, there is utter silence.*

*The murmur is coming from the frightened child, calling from somewhere deep within the heart of the swampland. Though he cannot see her, Killian Prophet knows that he is getting closer. As he staggers on, the murmur increases in clarity.*

*"Daddy, I'm so cold," Tressa whispers to his aching mind. "I'm so cold."*

*When Killian sees her in the distance, he leaps upon a thin layer of ice, breaking through to the frigid, shallow water beneath. He trudges across the short distance to crawl back up a steep embankment, ignoring the cold and his sprained ankle. His child is hanging by her feet from the snow-laden limb of a cypress tree.*

*"Hold on, Tressa," he shouts, "Daddy's coming!"*

*Killian is almost there, running with a painful limp that will not hinder him. The path winds right, and then veers to the left. He is so close now, panting as he maneuvers through the trees.*

*"Hurry, Daddy!" Tressa cries. "I'm afraid. I'm so cold!"*

*"I'm right here, Baby. Daddy's here," he says as he clears the last obstacle. Killian reaches for his daughter and freezes. His eyes stretch, and his chest seizes as he stumbles backward into the water. Tressa is hanging upside down, gently swaying back and forth. The rope around her ankles creaks wickedly.*

*Killian whimpers, "No. Oh God, no."*

*Tressa's eyes are open, but a thin layer of frost has formed on her purple skin. Her mouth stands agape as if to accuse, but no breath escapes her to cloud the chilly air. A red icicle has formed from the left corner of Tressa's lips. She is dead, long dead.*

*Broken and desolate, Killian shouts as he stumbled backward and slumps to his knees in the frigid water with his outstretched hands trembling in midair.*

Killian Prophet jerks out of the only sleep that he's had in days to find that Essie's car is still heading west. Burning tears well in his eyes as he clasps his hands together to pray, because nightmares become a horrible premonition of doom.

Sensing his pain, Essie takes his hand. She has a lump in her throat, wishing that she could say or do something to comfort him.

"Hurry," he says. "She's frightened."

Ten minutes later, after nearly skidding into a ditch, Essie leaves the highway. She drives for fifteen minutes along Parget Road, until they come upon a bright red phone booth that seems glaringly out of place.

"There isn't much time," Killian says.

As the car slides to a stop, he gets out on the run. The phone is ringing, but he hears a dial tone when he snatches the receiver from the hook. The desperate father fears that he is too late.

When it rings again, he grabs it and says, "I'm here. Hello. Is anyone there?"

After an agonizing moment of silence, the kidnapper's altered voice says, "Killian Prophet?"

"Yes. I'm here; now what?"

"Have you followed my instructions to the letter?"

"Yes. I just want my daughter to go home safe and sound. The authorities don't know that I left."

"You better be telling the truth. If I see anything out of order, your kid dies. Do you fucking understand me?"

"Understood. Please, let me speak to her. Let me speak to my daughter," Killian pleads.

There was another moment of silence. Then a small, sickly voice warns, "Daddy, please don't come. The bad men want to hurt you." Tressa is rocked by a rattling cough.

"I've got to, Baby. Daddy's got to come so you'll be safe."

"I'm so cold."

The phone is taken away, but Killian can still hear Tressa's miserable cough. His heart is breaking and his soul bleeds for her.

"Satisfied? Do exactly as I say and she'll be allowed to leave with your pretty little friend."

Killian's heart skips a beat when he realizes that the kidnappers are watching him. To the northwest, atop a hill, stands a structure that he cannot quite make out. He receives further instructions, reminded of the consequences of deviating from the route. Somehow he knows where the road will end.

The weatherman has predicted that another massive cold front will be coming from the northwest, reaching the area within the next twenty-four to forty-eight hours.

With the wheels crunching patches of snow and sheets of ice, they travel an old dirt track through a quiet woodland area. Atop the hill, Killian and Essie finally arrive at the old barn they saw from below. Surely animals are no longer kept in this place, for it looks haunted. The neglected red paint is peeling and faded. A hayloft door hangs slanted on a broken hinge. It looks as if it will fall off at any moment.

Essie's heart thuds and she breaks out in a sweat. Her headache pounds with renewed fury.

Killian looks to the hayloft above, feeling eyes upon them. He tells Essie that they are close enough, so she stops the car about thirty yards from the barn. The ground here is completely covered with snow. His breath is clearly visible when he gets out of the car.

With every silent second that passes, Killian's heart surges with anticipation. Just as he thinks it will explode from his chest, one of the large bay doors creaks open.

Someone comes out to take a precautionary look before allowing the child to walk into the cloudy light of day.

"Tressa," Killian whispers, as if he has not the strength to say her name any louder. She is dressed in her jeans and bed slippers, holding herself as if her little arms are frozen to her body.

Killian swallows hard when he notices the weapon pointed at her head. He glances back at Essie, certain that he will never lay eyes on her beautiful smile again. It has been something he longed for on quiet days and lonely nights.

He says, "I love you. Please take care of my little girl. You must not wait around when she gets here. Promise me that!"

With abject tears streaming down her face, Essie nods. She whispers her love for him with heart-heaving effort.

Killian walks toward the kidnappers, stopping halfway to await Tressa's release. The child now walks toward her dad with her eyes downcast and joyless because she understands his sacrifice. She shivers from the crown of her head to the soles of her feet. Behind her purple lips, her teeth chatter despite her will to stop them. She is despondent, distant, taking tiny shuffling steps in the snow.

Killian's and Essie's hearts go out to the child, who has suffered much. As she draws nearer, her father's feet and pant legs come into view. Her eyes rise from his knees to his hips and abdomen just as he removes his jacket. She sees his arms and hands rising to embrace her when he kneels in the snow.

As her father's arms surround her, the malicious voice from the barn causes Tressa to flinch. It warns, "Don't even think about running. There's a rifle aimed at her back and he'll kill her for sure!"

Tressa just stands there, unable to raise her arms to embrace her dad's neck as she dreamt about during her days of captivity. Killian looks into her eyes, seeing nothing of his nine-year-old daughter's fiery personality. She is like a ghost—lost between life, death, heaven . . . hell.

The desperate father cries, "Oh, Baby Girl, what have they done to you?" He looks over her shoulder and shouts, "What have you done to her?"

"Nothing compared to what we're gonna to do to you. The family reunion is over. Move it!"

"Go to the car, Tressa," Killian begs. "Please go with Essie, Sweetheart. She'll take you to your grandma and grandpa."

Tressa refuses to move—or perhaps she cannot. In slow motion, she finally raises her arms to embrace her father. She lays her head upon his shoulder and whispers, "They hate you so much. Why do they want to hurt you, Daddy? Why can't we go home together?" Her shiver rocks him to his soul, sinking his heart to a thousand fathoms.

"Because they're evil, Sweetheart, but God will make them pay. God will come for them."

Looking over his shoulder, his eyes beckon Essie, even though he insisted that she never leave the car. It is plain to see that the child will not go willingly.

Essie runs to Tressa, taking her from her father's arms. She is careful to keep Killian's jacket around Tressa's shoulders as he pries her arms from his neck.

Essie begs Killian to make a run for it, but she sees by his expression that he isn't willing to chance their safety.

He kisses Tressa's hot cheek and touches the matted locks of her hair. Then he kisses Essie on the lips and says, "Go now. Remember your promise."

With Tressa crying for Killian, Essie rushes to the car where the heater is on to warm the child.

A voice from the barn yells, "Move it, nigger!"

Killian faces his oppressors and walks his lonely mile, noticing that the man with the rifle is no longer visible in the loft. As Essie turns to leave, Killian hears a loud thump that seems to come from the barn. He pays it no attention while willing Essie and Tressa away from this dangerous place. When he looks back, the last thing he sees of them is Tressa's pale face and hands pressed against the window. They are finally gone.

Consigned to his fate with mere yards between them, Killian charges Sheriff Barnes. He intends to kill this man with his bare hands. Roscoe Barnes backs away. His movement is very nonchalant as he stops only inches inside of the door.

Killian quickly closes the gap. Just as he enters the door, a wooden bat meets his abdomen with a crushing blow! It cracks one of his ribs and he goes down hard. Both men attack.

A car starts behind the barn, tearing off toward the road. Through the raining blows, Killian looks up just in time to see the police cruiser's lights come on. That was what he heard—the door slamming shut.

He shouts, "You tricked me!" Fueled by rage, he tries to get up.

A nightstick crashes into Killian's stomach and then into his skull. He sees stars as blood spurts from his busted teeth and lips. He reaches for the door, but the lights go out. He has been woefully deceived.

Essie is tempted to make a quick stop to secure Tressa's seatbelt, but she manages the difficult task on the fly. A plea to return is written upon the child's face, etched into every fiber of her expression—an expression Essie avoids because her pain is so powerful.

As Essie Dantzler barrels down the country road, she promises, "Tressa, don't worry. We'll call the police with my cell phone and tell them . . ."

Essie twitches with her breath frozen in her lungs. Her head pounds when she notices a police car in the rearview mirror. Its lights are still in the distance when she recalls the FBI agents' theories. They believed that the culprits could be rogue police officers, badge-wearing racists who are not above murder and kidnapping.

She guns it.

The sloppy road conditions make it extremely difficult to control the car, but Essie can scarcely afford to slow down with the pursuer closing in.

She reaches inside of her coat pocket for her revolver, which she places between her thighs. This time, Essie vows to kill anyone who comes after the child. She is running for both their lives, almost close enough to smell the highway and the thinning possibility of freedom that it promises. The terrified woman forces the car on, weaving and yawing to get there quickly.

The cruiser is upon her, ramming Essie's bumper to ditch her car. Repeatedly he comes at her, unable to tap that sweet spot on either side because of the narrow track.

Anthony Barnes comes at her hard, but it is an ill-timed attempt. He hits her just as she turns the wheel to take the right fork in the road. Essie's car fishtails, but she struggles for control as the police car spins out of its orbit in the left fork. She sees a cloud of muddy snow flying in her mirror, but the car is no longer in pursuit.

Essie Dantzler races for safety, soon emerging from the dense woodland area. She begins to breathe easier and looks at the quiet child, fearing that Tressa may be on the verge of going into shock.

Just as Essie reaches for Tressa's sweating forehead, the police cruiser explodes onto the scene and rams her in the side. Front and side air bags inflate instantaneously, but to no avail. Suddenly and completely, silence fills the violent world.

With steam rising from the Volvo's underbelly, a yawning metallic cry escapes Tressa's door when Anthony Barnes tries to gain access.

He yanks at the door for the fourth time, forcing it open with foul language spewing from his bleeding lips. With little mercy, he releases the seatbelt that holds the unconscious child aloft and drags her from the car by the arm.

He liberates Essie Dantzler from the seatbelt and drags her out of the car by the hair. Her head is bleeding, but he feels no pity when he heaves her body onto the ditch bank. He then hauls them both to his bruised squad car, leaving four distinctive drag marks in the muddy snow.

In Myrtle Beach, Mayor Edward Renfrew makes a passionate public plea, asking listeners to come forward with any information they might have concerning the abduction of young Tressa Prophet. He condemns the kidnapping as a cruel and malicious act that has no place in today's society. When he's finished, a live feed airs from the Prophet home, where relentless reporters have camped.

It begins with a frenzied search by federal agents scouring the estate in search of Killian Prophet. A daring reporter and camera operator have sneaked onto the property by way of the beachfront, hiding behind the hedgerow that lines the wall that divides Killian's property from Essie Dantzler's home.

An agent bursts from a metal door on the north side of the Prophet home. The door looks like an entry to an ordinary storage area or auxiliary generator housing, but nothing more.

Other agents run from both the front and rear entrances after searching every inch of the house. The female agent emerges from that same door, joining Agent Lee, who points at what appears to be vanishing footprints in the snow.

They cross the short expanse and disappear through a gate that leads to the neighbor's yard, the same women who was in possession of Tressa Prophet when the abduction occurred.

The reporters attempts to retreat toward their point of entry so that they might get into Essie Dantzler's backyard. However, agents who search the grounds of Killian's estate spot them.

They are chased with the camera still running.

Just before they are apprehended, the cameraman captures a shot of Agents Lee and Siegle entering the neighbor's home from the rear.

Reporter Timothy Atkins says, "That was a live report from the home of the best-selling author, Killian Prophet, whose nine-year-old daughter was abducted in broad daylight here in Myrtle Beach approximately forty-eight hours ago. It would seem that federal agents at the Prophet home are now engaged in the frantic search for the writer and his neighbor, the woman who was brutally beaten by the child's alleged kidnappers."

Atkins looks at the monitor before saying, "WSCW correspondent Robby Page is presently at the scene. Rob, what do you make of all this?"

The camera goes live on location. "We're not certain of all the details, Tim. As you can see, there is a great deal of activity on the grounds and surrounding area of Killian Prophet's home. It would seem that Mr. Prophet has disappeared, along with his neighbor, Ms. Essie Dantzler. No one, including the FBI, seems to know where they are at this time. A moment ago I heard one of the men, and I assume that he's a member of the task force that's assigned to this case, asking who had seen the writer last. We'll be reporting the latest developments as the information becomes available. It seems that there is definitely more to this case than meets the eye. Back to you, Tim."

## CHAPTER 14

# Judgment

The writer's limp body is hoisted into the air by the handcuffs clamped mercilessly to his wrists. Because of his weight, they dig deeply into his swelling flesh to his bones.

When Killian's eyes finally open, his first instinct is to look about to see if he is alone. The taunting laughter that arises from the shadows tells him that he isn't.

He looks up to his hands, where every movement causes excruciating pain. Blood has dried like crimson icicles on his forearms.

As slow, ominous footsteps approach from the rear, Killian looks down at his right foot. He can do nothing, but his sneakers are still on his feet. When the footsteps halt, Anthony Barnes stands before Killian Prophet with a malicious grin.

"Who are you people?" he asks, realizing that he has lost a front tooth during the vicious attack. Bloody saliva spurts through the gap, running down his cracked lower lip, stinging him.

"Quite frankly, Mister, we're your worst nightmare come to life."

A car is approaching, but Anthony Barnes doesn't appear to worry that it might be the FBI. Killian quickly loses hope.

The cop has a stick in his hands, only it does not look like an ordinary piece of wood. In fact, it is made of plastic and rubber, crowned with dual metallic tips.

Anthony notices Killian's interest, so he drapes the cattle prod over his shoulder. With a smile, he casually strolls toward the stall door that stands directly before the captive author. "I couldn't help noticing that you seemed to hope that the approaching car might be the cops. You know what, Mr. Prophet? They probably are." He unlatches a stall door, allowing it to swing open on its squeaking hinges.

Killian's eyes bulge. "You tricked me. You never intended to let my daughter go. Why? She's innocent, for God's sake!" The car is closer and slowing down.

Anthony Barnes laughs at Killian's frustration. "Oh, we just wanted to have some fun with you. You didn't actually think we'd let them go so they could report our happy little gathering, did you?"

Killian says nothing as he stares down at the limp forms on a bed of straw. They are motionless, and it worries him greatly.

"Oh, they're not dead. Not yet, anyway," Anthony taunts. He kneels and places his hand on Tressa's feverish forehead. Her eyes do not open when he shakes her violently.

As expected, Killian reacts, so enraged that he ignores his many painful injuries. "Take your filthy hands off of her!"

Anthony Barnes chuckles. "You don't like that?" he asks. "Daddy's little girl is burning up. I'd say she's just about done for." He snatches a wad of Essie's hair in his grasp. "Hmm. So this is sugar daddy's big girl. Very nice, Mr. Prophet. Even though she's a little beat up, I might just sample me a taste. I'd like to see how the lower half lives. Maybe I can bone up on my sensitivity training."

"Leave them alone, you gutless prick!" Killian has deadly intent in his eyes, but he is helpless to carry out any threat.

"I don't like your tone, Mister!" Anthony Barnes approaches the captive and jabs him in the gut with the butt of the cattle prod. He swings it at the writer's midsection.

The sheriff's nasty younger brother is just warming up. He says, "This is for my little brother and cousin, you son of a bitch!"

He rams the cattle prod into the writer's right armpit and triggers the batteries. To his delight, the writer jitters about, unable to cry out through his clenched teeth. He pulls it away.

Once released from the grip of the electrical charge, Killian gasps for air.

Now, in a moment of sudden inspiration, Anthony asks, "What do you suppose will happen if I was to hit you in the balls with this prod? I heard that an electric charge like that could kill a fella. Let's test that theory, shall we?"

Killian kicks at his tormentor, sending him to the floor with a heel to the jaw. With fire in his eyes, Anthony quickly regains his feet.

"As God is my witness, you're all going to pay!" Killian shouts.

After wiping the dust from his face, Anthony says, "It looks like you're about to write your last chapter!" He advances with intention of carrying out the deathblow.

"Stop right there. Don't you kill the prisoner before his trial!" the old man says from the door.

Anthony Barnes freezes, looking like a kid caught with his hand in the cookie jar. He says, "Daddy, I was just having some fun."

"You were just about to kill our prisoner without due process," Judge Barnes says. "That's what you were doing."

"But I wasn't really gonna . . ."

"Don't perjure yourself with me, Boy. I've spent decades on the bench and I know a lie when I'm about to hear one."

Killian looks at the old man, whose words are holding this maniac at bay. He is, however, no more relieved to see Judge Barnes than he is to see Roscoe and Officer Baker, the two who beat him.

Once they are inside, Roscoe snatches the cattle prod from his brother's hand. He raises it as if he would smack Anthony in pretense.

"You're just a bloodthirsty, mad dog killer, aren't you, Tony."

Judge Barnes, using his cane for support, moves in for a closer inspection of the broken writer. With no feelings of remorse, he looks at the caged captives and grunts. It is about time to begin, so he aims his beautiful poison at the offending writer for whom he's cultivated such contempt that a son of his has perished in its pursuit.

The retired judge stands about seven feet from the dangling writer, adjusts his glasses, and straightens his black robe. He says, "I'm Judge Benjamin Barnes. These two men are my sons, Sheriff Roscoe Barnes and Deputy Officer Anthony Barnes. This here is Deputy Officer Baker. Now, I'm telling you this out of no sense of moral obligation, other than the fact that a man should know death's name when he's staring it down the pike. You should concede to the inevitable fact that you are going to be executed, Sir. This hearing is but a formality."

The room is still spinning for Killian. The pain in his wrists is the only thing that keeps him from passing out. It is bad enough to come crashing through his nerve endings, but not enough to make his brain retreat into unconsciousness.

He focuses on Judge Barnes to ask, "Why me? I never laid eyes on you people in my life. Why have you murdered my wife and kidnapped my innocent child? Why? What could I have possibly done to make you hate me so much?"

Barnes tilts his glasses to look directly into the black man's eyes and says, "You murdered my youngest son about two years ago. Don't you remember that?"

Killian is enraged at the absurdity of that statement. "It was self-defense, damn it. They broke into my home and attacked my family without provocation. I didn't know that they existed until they tried to draw first blood."

"Silence. I order you to be silent in my court, or I'll find you in contempt!" Officer Baker looks at Judge Barnes, dubiously. This was almost funny to him.

"I will not be silent. You attacked us, and now I stand accused, condemned for defending my family against your assassins. Do you honestly think that you can justify the murder of my wife and the kidnapping of my daughter? Fuck you all to hell!"

"I hold you in contempt, Sir. Your punishment will be swiftly administered. Bailiff, show him who is boss here!"

Roscoe drives his fist into Killian's gut, then hits him with a charge from the cattle prod. The writer jerks about, gritting his teeth against the repeated electro-shock!

As sweat begins to run down Killian's forehead, the torture abates. Sheriff Barnes steps back, watching as the writer's eyes flutter.

"Now then, I suppose you'll be a bit more agreeable and respectful of this court of law," Judge Barnes states.

Killian holds onto consciousness to whisper, "Please. I beg for mercy. My daughter and Essie are innocent, Your Honor. Let them go and I'll throw myself on the mercy of the court."

"You fail to see that you're already at the mercy of the court," the judge scoffs. "Let the record show that the defendant's plea for leniency is denied!"

Killian shouts, "They attacked us for no reason. Your fucking son broke into my home to murder my entire family!"

"No, Sir. They were not there to murder, but to execute the sentence handed down by the court. He was sent to silence a trouble-maker, to quell the supporters of race-mixing and other evils that are abominations before the Lord God. Your perverted ideals are dangerous propaganda that we must not permit to grow like the cancer that it is!"

Defiantly, Killian shouts, "What the hell are you talking about? You're fucking mad!"

Holding true to his nature, Judge Barnes is offended. "Bailiff, you may silence the defendant as you see fit!"

Anthony Barnes joins the sheriff in pummeling Killian Prophet. He takes the nightstick from his belt and winds up as if receiving a pitch. After hitting homer after homer, he raises the club over his head and brings it down, slamming the lead-filled wood into Killian's right knee.

Simple reflex causes the writer to draw his battered leg up to his chest, where it would not stay. Just as it goes limp, the club delivers another bone-crushing blow. Though the club misses Killian's raised leg, it finds his abdomen with vengeance.

Baker steps forward at this point to slam his fist into Killian's face. The author coughs, ejecting another tooth and blood from his mouth and nostrils. Then Baker uses his Taser. When it is finally over, Killian is dazed, swooning on the edge of physical oblivion.

Judge Barnes says, "Keep it up and you won't live until tomorrow night's gathering. Now then, I will read the damning evidence." He reaches back to raise his robe, taking a copy of one of Killian's first novels from his back pocket. The paperback is bookmarked.

When Judge Barnes brandishes the cover of *Dark Eclipse*, he asks, "Does the defendant recognize the evidence brought forth by the prosecution? Does he?"

Killian nods his head to confirm, fearing their wrath.

"Is the defendant not responsible for the following quotations?" He reads, "They are useless stumbling blocks in what future paths may lay before the whole of mankind. They are absolute in their smallish thinking, wasting amongst the weeds of animosity in the midst of dark swamps. They are proving woodland convictions where animals other than themselves may never protest their fouling of this land." Judge Barnes turns the page and resumes. 'They are concealed by masks of cowardly acts during dark time hours, knowing that the world wishes not to see them thrive nor prosper because their resurgence heralds humanity's regression and defeat. They've truly become the minority, and as such, we now have the greater power to seek them out and disband the quiet evil that easily infects the innocent." Judge Barnes looks at Killian for a second.

Killian stares back at him with utter disdain.

"'Until we have removed all barriers of race, physicality, and social intolerance, the Ku Klux Klan and other such institutions of ignorance and malice will remain blights upon all that we might become as a nation of diverse cultures. Then, and only then, may we truly aspire to become what God envisioned of his seed. Their misguided cause is brutal and petulant, but they cannot be ignored while burrowing deep to reinvent their many means of terror. I will seek out and eliminate them from the roots to the highest limbs of a cancerous tree that shrouds us in darkness. On bended knees, I bow down to seek God's mercy upon my soul, for it is my decree that I will hunt them down whithersoever they may reside. I shall slay them all one by one, until mine own soul drowns in their blood, for God is a power everlasting. Many will judge my deeds evil, but I am sent from above to rein down on the contemptuous as Almighty God's avenging angel. Amen and amen!'"

For a moment, Judge Barnes scowls at Killian Prophet in silence.

"That . . ." Killian says. ". . . that is from a book of fiction. It's just a story, but you're completely missing the point. That character's way of thinking is no better than . . ."

"So you do admit recognition. Let the record reflect the defendant's admission of guilt."

"What's that got to do with anything?" Killian says in barely a whisper. "I made it all up."

Within, he agonizes over the fact that his loving wife was murdered because of something he wrote. To have only suspected was bad enough, but to know is utterly dreadful. Judge Barnes has just recited the fictitious ravings of a black madman, whose hatred and thirst for revenge destroyed him in the end.

Killian is nearly undone by the sudden answer to his and Tressa's question of why those evil men came in the night to destroy their happy, prosperous lives.

As morbid tears fall from his burning eyes, Prophet looks to the sky and asks, "Why, God? Why?"

"You write as if you are the emissary of God, but today the only god you need concern yourself with is probably standing right before you," Judge Barnes snaps.

"It is just a story. A freaking fairytale," Killian says.

"No, Sir—this is a formal and blasphemous declaration of war!" Now Judge Barnes continues to read. "'Tonight I go to Conway, where the devil resides. By my soul, I shall not leave that place until the rivers run red with their blood and the blood of their accursed children. They are judgment, but I am wrath!'"

Killian shouts, "Fiction. Fucking fiction!"

"War, that's what it is. Black on white crimes rose fifty percent since this garbage was first printed. You cannot realize the negative connotations of what you've written about my town and its people. Who told you such things? What do you know of us? Answer me, damn it!" Judge Barnes has become hoarse from the shouting.

"It's fucking fiction. I swear to God in heaven, that's all it is. Nothing more."

"Are you trying to tell me that you've never heard of a man named Reverend Richard Drover? You've never heard of the feud that uppity Negro had with my daddy, Cole Barnes?"

"What the fuck are you talking about?" Killian asks in bewilderment. "I've never heard of either."

"Let the record show that this lying sack of shit has denied any knowledge. It is funny that you claim to know nothing of my family history when it's clear that you used some of the very words that bastard preacher used before he murdered my father fifty years ago. Now how is it possible for you to have written these things nearly word for word? Who have you been talking to in Conway? Answer me, Boy!"

For the first time, Killian sees them clearly. If the situation were not so serious, he may have laughed at that old man's sheer paranoiac lunacies. It is all so ridiculous that it actually begins to make perfect sense. This entire tragedy has been sparked by some ironic coincidence. He just picked the wrong town to mess with, a town he'd never even visited. It was only chosen from a short list of possible scenes because of location, its plot feasibility, and because of the way it sounded when it rolled off the tongue. Conway. Because of these small things, his family suffered miserably. What a terrible price they paid for the value of absolutely nothing.

"You're all fucking crazy. You're as crazy as a cowbell on a fucking horse," Killian says in defiance. "I am far from perfection, Mister, but I am a righteous man. My child and woman are innocent. If any harm comes to us, if we should all perish at your hands, then I promise you that I will rain down on you from heaven. And we will return—the four of us—to tear your measly little lives asunder as an utmost favor to God Almighty himself!"

Judge Barnes is inflamed, and the writer's insolence will not go unpunished. "Silence him!"

"This, I vow. You hear me, you crazy son of a bitch? This I vow!"

Anthony Barnes snatches the cattle prod from Roscoe's hand and drives it at the writer's genitals. Its furious spark causes such pain that brings an agonizing cry from Killian's lips. Then, as suddenly as it begins, there is nothing. His head simply slumps forward.

"The verdict is in. We the people do find the defendant guilty of all charges. His sentence is death, which will be carried out no later than tomorrow night. At that time, the defendant and all those who would continue his blasphemy will be put to death before a gathering of men that he will never hope to peer. It is so adjudged!"

Thirty minutes following his trial, Prophet's accusers return to Judge Barnes's house to discuss an unsavory development.

Anthony Barnes has been dating Ray Lampoon's secretary, Cheryl Grant, for the past two months. Cheryl unwittingly mentioned a need for better employment, where repetition isn't always necessary. She told him that she is tired of making two and three copies of everything. She is always expected to reproduce at least two hard copies of every invoice, contract, bill receipt, data disk, file, and photo. She calls it "Hi-Lo Tech."

Ms. Grant told Anthony Barnes that she stumbled across files in Lampoon's open safe one day, when she was looking to steal some petty cash. She needed some gas and lunch money, so she peeked when he was in the bathroom with a bad case of the runs. She discovered pictures of that black writer everyone was talking about. She paid it little attention until the writer's kid was snatched. The woman wants to know if there is a reward for that sort of information because she suspects Ray Lampoon of having something to do with it.

It appears that Lampoon is holding out on the sheriff, who has commissioned him to do all of the legwork in his family's obsession with Killian Prophet. The first time was two years ago, when Lampoon was told that Killian Prophet was suspected of running drugs into Conway via the river systems. After the first attempt on Killian's life, however, Lampoon knew better. In fact, his initial investigation of the man disturbed him greatly. Prophet, a successful writer, displayed none of the characteristics of a drug lord. He seemed to have no motivation to involve himself with trafficking.

After Miranda Prophet's murder, there was a confrontation between Roscoe Barnes and Ray Lampoon, who were once close friends with very similar racial attitudes. But Lampoon changed in many ways over the years. Things had happened in his life to uproot his basic prejudices and intolerance.

Lampoon's youngest sister died of a drug overdose, so taking the first case was not a problem for him. However, shadowing Killian Prophet two years ago did more to prove him innocent rather than guilty of drug trafficking. Every fiber in Lampoon's being warned him then that there must be more to their interest in this writer. He had all of the evidence, but no clue as to what they actually had in store for the man.

The second job, which included investigating the parents of Killian's bodyguards and his neighbor, was done under extreme duress. Everything, right down to Margo Firestone's phone number, he had given them with threats hanging over his head, like a razor-sharp pendulum on a corroded chain.

Little did Sheriff Barnes know that Lampoon's attitudes toward blacks had changed drastically since high school and his days on the force. Lampoon was enthusiastic about bringing down a drug kingpin. Truthfully, it would not have mattered to him if Prophet had been a white man.

He invaded an innocent man's privacy, handing over complete files of Prophet's dealings and movements, which were then used in a criminal act by vigilante cops.

By holding onto evidence, Ray Lampoon proved that he cannot be trusted. Someone would have to take care of him, but Sheriff Barnes has other matters to attend.

CHAPTER 15

# The Profile

*P*acing before the tactical board, Agent Lee vents frustration. "How the hell did we lose him?" He reaches for his cup of tea, but decides that he's had enough.

"His literary agent delivered the message. I'm getting a warrant to have her phone records pulled as we speak. If we get lucky, we'll have our point of reference," Agent Siegle replied.

"I should have that woman brought up on obstruction charges," Lee says.

"What good will it do? She was afraid to do other than instructed, and Prophet made her promise to keep quiet. She is more than just his agent, Anjon—she became the child's godmother after Miranda Prophet was murdered. That's a heavy responsibility, and any number of people would have done the same," says Siegle. She is equally upset, but she understands Margo's motive.

"Now you know why I've always insisted that only immediate family be allowed in the home. There are too many variables added when that rule is not strictly observed," Agent Lee declares. "Okay, let's see. What other avenues should we investigate? Let's have the downtown phone booth dusted for prints. Maybe we'll get lucky, but I doubt it. The kidnappers wouldn't have taped an envelope under the phone without wearing gloves. They're certainly too clever for that."

"We'll probably find that the text was sent from a disposable prepaid phone that has no registered owner. But why didn't they just send the picture of the child with the text? Why tape it inside a phone booth?"

"According to Margo's description of the photo and the time involved, I don't think they took it in the van before discarding it," Agent Lee says while looking away from his partner.

"You think that someone took the Polaroid and brought it back once they were secure?"

"Makes sense to me."

"This investigation is in deep trouble," Siegle says.

Agent Lee sighs. "Mr. Prophet, you have no idea what you've done."

"I believe he knows exactly what he's gotten himself into by now. He chose to sacrifice himself for Tressa's sake, but he was desperate enough to rely on the word and honor of murderers and kidnappers, who promised to release the child once they had him. He made the same choice that almost any parent would. He was the target all along. That much we know."

Lee taps a pointer on the tactical board, thinking hard. He asks, "But why? Angela, you're a fan of his, aren't you?"

"I believe I've read everything he's ever had published," she says. "Why do you ask?"

"I know he's reputed to be one of the best black writers in this country, but I've never really read his work. Exactly what kind of a writer is he?"

Angela Siegle rubs her knotted neck, pacing before the bookshelf. She pauses for a moment to consider the titles, touching the binding of *Dark Eclipse*, a story about an insane black man whose family was murdered by racists.

"He's deep," she says with admiration. "The imagination it must take to write like he does is way beyond me. I used to write stories when I was in high school and college, but I wasn't very good at it because I always got hung-up on details that meant very little in the end. I never got anything published, but not for a lack of trying. However, Killian Prophet—the Black Assassin—is a master at what he does. Prophet makes you feel it. His books, no matter what the subject matter, can take you from sidesplitting laughter to tears. He is a talent and a credit to the literary world. He's very deep."

"What do you mean by that?"

"Prophet gets to the root of human disease. Many of his books encompass racism as the central theme, but he's not fixated—at least, I don't think so. He doesn't come off like some angry black man with a giant chip on his shoulder, though I'm sure that some people would disagree. His work is fictional, with the exception of his latest. However, I always get the feeling that his stories could easily be based upon events that have actually happened, or might have. He started an entirely new genre, if you ask me. You have love stories, human-interest stories, mystery and suspense . . . and horror stories. In most cases, Prophet combines these elements to create what I consider to be social horror. He's hardly written about monsters, the childhood beast-under-the-bed variety— he mostly writes about the human kind."

Anjon Lee says, "Hmm. I suppose that's what I'm more interested in."

"When you start a Killian Prophet novel, whether you like the subject matter or not, you're dragged kicking and screaming to the very last syllable. Since I have no life of my own, I read. On my days off, I've often found myself up at four or five in the morning. Sometimes, if you want the truth, reading with all of the lights on."

"So he doesn't sugar-coat. He attacks the real life monster, the kind that preys on innocence."

"The buzz is that two of his novels are slated for the big screen. His agent is presently engaged in contract negotiations with Paramount and MGM. In addition, when you asked me how much he was worth, originally, I was misinformed. He's worth quite a bit more." Angela Siegle begins to pull Killian's collection of books from the shelf. She stacks them next to her computer.

"I see that we're thinking alike again, Angela. You may just be the woman of my dreams," Agent Lee teases.

"It's just too bad that you're married. Otherwise, Old Man, I'd rock your Asian-American world," she says. They smile at each other.

"What if Killian Prophet accidentally offended some real life monsters in one of these books? What if he just happened to cut too close to the bone and caused someone to pay him special attention?" Agent Lee wonders.

She says, "It's a long shot. But if it's true, then it would stand to reason that a clue is in one of these novels."

"I'll call headquarters and have the thinkers put on this immediately," Lee says. "The real computer geeks might have a different take."

"Meanwhile, at the risk of you becoming a fan yourself, we'll work on these. We have to cross-reference the racist profiles, their places of origin, and event horizons. The answer may be in here . . . somewhere. Actually, I know it is," she says. Agent Lee calls headquarters.

Killian's parents are upstairs, talking to an anxious Margo First. They are more worried than ever, but she has concerns of her own. A bit disheveled, Margo says, "I hate to be so self absorbed, I really do. You're an attorney, Andy. Do you think they will bring charges against me? They were furious." Margo wrings her sweating hands.

Anders looks at his wife, who is upset with both of them. Ethyl's eyes cut him to the quick—and when Margo confronts that icy gaze, she wishes she could just disappear.

With fire and condemnation spewing from her heart, Ethyl Prophet declares, "They should lock you both away for what you've done!"

"Ethyl!" Anders cries in disbelief.

"Don't you Ethyl me. You two fools have sent our son to his death, and you damn well know it. They may all die because of your decision to keep quiet!" she shouts.

Anders says, "We don't know that for sure. Killian is very resourceful." He knows that his wife's angry eyes are close to tears.

Margo makes the mistake of approaching Ethyl Prophet in her moment of fear and anger. It is quickly clear to Margo that Ethyl's anger is more prevalent.

"Take your hands off of me, Bitch, or I swear by God Almighty . . . I'll cut you down!"

Margo retreats in the face of the woman's wrath. She moves toward the window, where she holds herself as if the temperature in that room has plummeted. Anders goes to her and explains that Ethyl was just upset and that she did not really mean the mean-spirited things she said.

They are exhausted, having been questioned over and again since Killian's disappearance. Their nerves are frazzled, tormented by the uncertain fate of three people who do not deserve such a tragic drama.

When Ethyl calms a bit, Anders sits beside her. She finally allows her husband of thirty-seven years to put his arms around her heaving shoulders. As she weeps in his arms, she cries, "I'm sorry, Andy. I'm just angry because I didn't get to say goodbye."

"I know, Ethyl. I know."

"What they must be going through right now!"

Someone is coming. He hears footsteps crunching in the snow, but it is hard to open his eyes. A person dressed in black drags the unconscious child from the cage and stretches her out on the cold, dusty floor before her father. He is wearing an executioner's hood.

The man in black slaps the writer to rouse him. Standing before the child, facing Killian, his voice is raspy when he says, "Such procedures require that a witness be present. That's you, Prophet." He laughs. "And her punishment is a death by decapitation!"

With his feet apart, the man in black raises a gleaming bush knife over his head.

Killian kicks and strains against his bonds, pleading for his daughter's life, to no avail.

As he cries "No," the blade slices through the air, making a perfect downward arch to sever her head from her still body. Blood gushes all over Killian's sneakers as Tressa's head rolls beneath his feet. His daughter's eyes open and blood spurts from her mouth!

The killer's wicked, mean-spirited laughter resonates throughout the hollow barn. His mockery echoes to mingle with the tormented author's screams.

Finally, mercifully, Killian Prophet's eyes roll upward as he faints dead away. Before he goes, that raspy voice echoes in his mind, "Your woman is next. She's next!"

## CHAPTER 16

# Lampoon

*T*he female reporter adjusts her collar and clears her scratchy throat. As she wonders if the dreary weather is bringing on a cold, she looks at the sky before taking her cue.

"This is Tammy Burch with a live Channel Five News report. I am presently at the home of Killian Prophet, in Myrtle Beach, South Carolina. If you've been following this tragic story, then you know that the nine-year-old daughter of the best-selling author has been abducted. Sources say that the authorities have made little or no headway in breaking this case. Because there has been no word from the kidnappers for at least forty-eight hours, Prophet family members had begun to fear the worst. Then, in a strange twist of fate, Killian Prophet suddenly disappeared, along with his neighbor, the same woman who was in temporary custody of the child when the alleged kidnapping took place. Many people are speculating on the reasons behind Mr. Prophet's sudden disappearance, but I'm sorry to say that some of those theories have been surprisingly negative. We have with us retired federal agent Cameron Penn. Mr. Penn, once a task force commander, dealt specifically with this kind of case." She turns to her left. "Mr. Penn, can you shed any light on this situation? Do you have any theories of your own?"

The fifty-eight-year-old man brushes a lock of silver hair from his forehead. "I really wouldn't put much stock in conjecture and rumors, Ms. Burch. Since I arrived, I've heard some ghastly theories. One person even said that Mr. Prophet and his neighbor might have staged the child's kidnapping, that they ran away because the FBI was close to finding them out. To suggest something like that is not only ignorant and very irresponsible, but also cruel and malicious. The writer most likely received some kind of covert communication from the kidnappers, who know that the FBI will be involved in such a high-profile case. Based on what happened to his family a couple of years ago, I'd say that these are the same people or the same type. That being said, Mr. Prophet has probably been their objective all along. People are out there spreading rumors and half-truths that probably have no basis in fact, but this family has been deeply hurt because of what the kidnappers have done. Unfortunately, we're living in an imperfect world, where people harm innocent children to get at the parents."

Ms. Burch asks, "What do you think will be the probable outcome of this situation, Mr. Penn?"

"Mr. Prophet has probably gone to trade himself for his daughter. If that's the case, I'm afraid he has fallen for one of the oldest tricks in the book. It's a brave and noble thing to do, but very foolish. Any loving parent would gladly lay down his or her life for their child. That's a given. Ultimately, Mr. Prophet has given these predators complete control by evading his best hope, which is the federal team of investigators. I hope and pray that I'm wrong, but they're all probably doomed."

The reporter asks, "On what do you base this assumption?"

He sighs. "On my many years of experience at the bureau." A tear slides from Penn's eye. He places his hands in his pocket when they begin to shake. "These cases are the worst, when innocent children are used against their parents by people who hate so furiously that the end justifies the means. This is another sad day in American history. May God forgive them for this."

Penn looks to the ground in earnest shame before walking to his car.

Angela Siegle rubs her tired eyes. "What's Penn doing down here?" she asks with a bit of hostility in her voice.

"He lives nearby. Been here since retirement," Agent Lee replies.

"I see."

"No—maybe you don't," Lee snaps. "He's got nothing to do with the investigation. More than likely, someone dug him up for an educated guess. So leave him alone and concentrate on this angle of ours, because I believe it holds merit."

"You're right. I'm sorry," she says, a little chagrined.

"No need to apologize, Angela. I understand your feelings. You were right six years ago. He was very wrong, and it cost someone's life. Now, let it go."

She almost smiles, but then she experiences a measure of remorse. To refocus her thoughts, Angela Siegle reins in her emotions.

Cameron Penn was once one of the best, a dedicated agent who had gotten long in the tooth. Because he got too close to his cases, the weight of success versus failure had aged and broken him. He retired a hero in some circles, but a miserable disappointment in others.

Deep down, Agent Lee hopes to end his career on a better note than his former partner. It was his main reason for giving up alcohol as an end-of-the-day fallback. He shakes his head at the television as Penn gets into his vehicle to drive away.

The stations next featured interview is with the wife of a police officer who is in recovery after a bank robber's bullet left him paralyzed from the neck down. Agent Lee turns the television off.

The story, however, sparks something in Agent Siegle. She puts the novel down and keys her computer, trying to urge a memory to the surface. Something she saw in the first case file, perhaps.

When Agent Lee's phone rings, he takes a call that he expected to come sooner. Upon hanging up, he sighs long and hard while pinching the bridge of his nose.

He says, "That was Assistant Director Gregory. He's under pressure from the governor to replace us. The good governor has requested that they scrap us and hand this case to the Hate Crimes Division, or make this a joint investigation. Either way would mean our subjugation."

"HCD had the investigation two years ago and got nowhere. What makes them think that they'll solve this one?" Agent Siegle asks with a bit of hostility. "They want a little redemption?"

"Gregory is in our corner, so I wouldn't sweat over it. He's going to keep the dogs at bay for as long as he can, but we have to make a difference."

"'When time is the enemy, the weather always turns bad.'"

"What?" he asks.

"It's just something I read in one of Killian's stories. 'When time is the enemy, the weather always turns bad.' It's snowing again." They got back to work.

Moments later, Agent Davis comes in with a video camera. He shows them the tape of Tammy Burch handing money to a police officer behind her news van. The two then shared a passionate kiss and parted, not knowing they were being watched.

Agent Lee calls the officer's precinct with venom in his voice. Even though the officer will not admit guilt, he is suspended for leaking information pertinent to a federal case.

The darkness of his dream is an ugly, desolate thing. As Killian ascends from the depths of sleep, a spider crawls toward him from some distant, shadowy realm. It is as if he's lain his head upon a table, looking directly at the creature while its eight legs propel it toward his face. As the spider approaches, a whitish haze engulfs it like a radiant aura. When its many legs became only four, its fangs became the white teeth of a grinning human being.

Killian's vision begins to clear. Sheriff Barnes is glaring up at the helpless writer with impunity, wearing a malicious grin as he rapes Killian's unconscious girlfriend.

Prophet's ragged mind is forced to attention as the man who murdered his wife and world lay atop Essie Dantzler.

Tressa, alive but not well, is kneeling in the cage. Her wide eyes do not blink. Her knuckles seem glued to the bars of the cage. Her breath comes in small, rapid puffs. Her skin is pallid and she coughs, painfully. Pneumonia is killing her body, while her dad's evil tormentor seeks to murder her young mind.

Killian looks down at his feet, where he sees the life-sized doll the executioner used to torture him. The realization that Tressa is still alive will bring him a warped moment of joy and pain, because the child is petrified, watching from a bird's eye view as Roscoe takes Essie Dantzler.

"Tressa, look away. Please look away, Sweetheart! Please close your eyes for Daddy. Baby, please look away," Killian pleads.

With little feeling other than the pain in his arms, Killian sneers at Roscoe Barnes. His swollen hands grip the iron bar overheard as he fights to dislodge its framework. His threats are an impotent string of profanity.

Sheriff Barnes says, "Even cold, she's still got some good pussy." He finally reaches his grunting orgasm to complete the act of debasing Killian's lover. With his eyes closed, he licks his lips, enjoying the feeling as he shudders and quakes. When it's over, the good sheriff looks over his shoulder at Tressa with a smile.

"You filthy . . ."

Still panting, Roscoe says, "What are you complaining about, Prophet? I bet you and your wife used to fuck in front of your kid all the time." He laughs as he withdraws from her. Barnes gets dressed while facing the child, but her eyes never leave Essie's violated body.

As Killian glares at Roscoe, he recognizes the bullet wounds. There is scar tissue on his shoulder and hip where the doctor patched him up. This is when Killian realizes that Roscoe Barnes is the man who got away two years ago, the man who murdered Miranda.

He growls, "You'd better kill me, Motherfucker. You'd better kill me soon!"

Essie moans from that lightless place where the concussion has taken her. She knows nothing of what this vile person has done to her, this man who swore an oath to protect and serve.

"Well, what do you know?" Roscoe says while looking down at Essie. "It looks as if she's finally coming around to my way of thinking, moaning and groaning like that. I think she liked it. Maybe she wants some more. You know, Prophet, I believe we just might have made us a little baby zebra."

"Get away from her!" Killian demands.

"Or what? What will you do, Prophet?" Roscoe asks as he cinches his belt. He draws his gun and points it at Essie's skull. "Or what?"

Tressa makes a low, moaning sound.

Killian struggles to be free, to no avail. His hands are swelling beyond the use of his numb fingers. In this private hell, he would gladly trade his very soul to Satan to see Barnes dead.

Before Roscoe walks away, he stands before Killian and says, "I see that you recognized my scars. Yes, I did enjoy blowing that bitch in half. However, you may rest assured that your troubles will soon be over and you'll be free to join her. Both halves of her."

As their eyes lock, Sheriff Barnes slaps Killian for good measure. When he kicks at the sheriff, he quickly regrets it.

Though his pain is monstrous, he raises his eyes to his terrified child and then again to Roscoe's wicked smile. Killian declares, "I swear by all that's holy, I will see you all burn in hell for what you've done. I swear to God, you will burn, Motherfucker!"

Roscoe slams his fists into Killian's gut until the writer is silent and his head finally slumps in unconsciousness.

As Roscoe Barnes is leaving, he drags Essie back into the cage by the hair. She is still wearing her blouse, but he neglects to pull her blue jeans and panties up.

Roscoe looks down at Tressa, whose eyes are anchored at his

knees. He grunts as he notices the burning beads of sweat that run down her forehead, but feels nothing.

When the cage door slams shut, she flinches. After Sheriff Barnes is out of her sight, Tressa's eyes slowly fall. Without looking down, she pries her right hand from the cold bar to cover her father's near-naked girlfriend with straw.

It is no small task for her to raise her eyes and look upon her dad. She sheds tears for him while praying before forcing herself to lie down next to Essie, where it is somewhat warmer.

The child is lost, paying a grownup's price in a grownup's war. In the wounded company of those loved most, she is so lost and alone. Tressa is surrounded by the whistling wind. However, other than this sound, there is silence, a dreadfully hollow . . . silence.

Anthony Barnes stares straight into Ray Lampoon's eyes a nanosecond before he draws his weapon. What he does not expect is a shotgun blast that obliterates the desk to send him backward. Most of the buckshot is annulled by the bulletproof vest, but he is hit in the left leg and hand by the burning pellets and wooden shards. The blast slams him against the wall near the office door.

Lampoon draws the sawed off double-barrel from the swivel beneath the desk. He points it at Anthony's head, pulling the trigger on a dud. He drops it on the desk, going for his handgun.

Anthony Barnes pulls the trigger of his automatic as he goes down. Lampoon is propelled into the wall on his rolling chair. The windowpanes shatter beside him.

Barnes regains his feet, aiming his weapon behind the desk to finish the job. Lampoon's blood is on the shattered glass and the wall, but there is no body.

Somehow, amidst the flying bullets and gunpowder, Lampoon has slipped away. His laptop is gone from the surface of the desk, but it goes unnoticed.

Anthony Barnes curses rotten luck. He holds the burning silencer, replacing one kind of pain with another. The youngest living Barnes limps away unseen.

CHAPTER 17

# *Conway*

gent Siegle is on fire. She pulls a tack from the board and sticks it into the new target area. She is living an emotion that all true geniuses experience when something so simple, so obvious, has escaped them. The light that blooms in her mind forces her to remember the day her college roommate walked into the dorm room and caught her staring at her feet. Angela's sneakers were between those size sixes, but she was engrossed in the debate over which was left and right. It was a particularly embarrassing moment back then, but nothing of importance had depended upon it. Even so, it became a point of reference for self-ridicule.

She mutters, "Conway, South Carolina! That has to be it. How could I have forgotten?"

Siegle digs into a faded memory, backtracking an Internet story about the wounded police officer who survived an armed attack by Mexican drug-runners. The sheriff's father, retired Judge Benjamin Barnes, saved his life by taking him to the hospital before he bled to death.

The modest Sheriff Roscoe Barnes barely survived his multiple gunshot wounds, only to face hours of major surgery.

The description of the wounds fit perfectly with Killian Prophet's post-breakdown recollection of the attack in Wilmington Beach.

This police officer was hailed as a hero. In a follow-up investigation, the immigrant shooters were supposedly killed while resisting arrest during what appeared to be a routine traffic stop.

Reportedly, the four suspects fired upon local law enforcement officers when surrounded. Only one of the arresting officers suffered injuries, but the gunmen were all killed when members of the Conway Sheriff's Department responded with justifiable deadly force.

After cross-referencing the date of the Internet article with justice department records of the officer's shooting, Agent Siegle looks at the sleeping Agent Lee. One of Killian Prophet's novels, *Dark Eclipse*, rests parted on his chest.

With both hands on her hips, Agent Siegle flexes her neck to make her stiff joints crackle. Standing before the board, she studies the map, testing her primitive theory. At the same time, she struggles to contain and direct her excitement.

By tracing the Intracoastal Waterway from Wilmington, North Carolina, she discovers a route from Killian's former home to the Waccamaw River, which leads directly to Conway, South Carolina. Miranda Prophet's murderer arrived and escaped by water. Conway was the focal point of Killian's novel, *Dark Eclipse*, which was reputed to be the bloodiest and most thought provoking work of fiction he'd written at that point in his career.

With a new day approaching, Angela Siegle traces the birth records of the two men killed by Killian Prophet at the Wilmington Beach murder scene. The puzzle begins to come together. The birth record of one of them leads to marriage records. The forensic DNA report indicates that the person who got away was closely related to one of those killed by Prophet two years ago. The answer has been there all along, but someone dropped the ball.

With dawn upon her, she wakes Agent Lee from his muchneeded sleep. As he emerges from unconsciousness, he surprises her by muttering, "Conway."

The novel falls from his chest, but she catches it. He'd fallen asleep on the very page where a black lunatic threatened to go after the devils in Conway as God's avenging angel.

Moments later, she concludes her tale by saying, "Theory fits the profile only if the profile fits the theory. You were convinced that the perpetrators could be cops from the beginning. One of the men that Killian killed has something in common with the heroic Sheriff Barnes—their mother. It fits like a glove, because Barnes may well be the one that got away from Wilmington Beach. Look here. The officer who received minor injuries during the shootout with the four so-called Mexican drug-running gunmen was none other than Officer Anthony Barnes, the sheriff's youngest surviving brother. He suffered a flesh wound that was probably self-inflicted."

Agent Lee says, "They were covering it up. The four young men they killed were probably framed to take the fall for Sheriff Barnes's shooting. They were murdered. It's not much, but yes—theory fits the profile only if the profile fits the theory. We better call the chopper." He grabs the phone and says, "Good work, Angela."

"Thanks. You should drink coffee from now on. It keeps you awake a lot longer than tea," she says with a smile. "It could happen to anyone, so don't beat yourself up about it. That's my job."

He feels a bit of guilt and shame, but she's right. They've been going full bore from the start of this mess. He fell asleep on the very page where the answer might have been found, but only because he's human.

*"The other six puppies of the litter seem to be jealous. They are climbing all over each other at the gate, whimpering for a bit of the affection Tressa showers on her pick. She kneels on the ground, smiling as the pup tickles her face with his whiskered muzzle and rough tongue.*

*Killian smiles to himself before asking, "So what are you going to name him?"*

*Tressa's smile disappears, as if his question is one of utmost seriousness. She takes a doggy treat from her pocket and gives it to the pup to divert its attention.*

*"What's the matter, Tressa?"*

*She looks up and asks, "Daddy, should we try to forget? Should we make everything new?"*

*Killian joins her on the ground. He pets the pup, looking directly into his daughter's eyes with great concern. "What do you mean, Sweetheart?"*

*"I mean, like Mommy?"*

*Killian nods, understanding her train of thought. He forces a smile and says, "No, Sweetheart. We should never forget your mother, no matter how much it hurts at times. Her love for us is eternal, Tressa, and we should always remember what she meant to us. I tried to forget once. Do you remember when I was in the hospital for so long?"*

*"Yes, Sir."*

*Well, because I felt it was somehow my fault, and it hurt so much to think that way, I forgot everything that was good about our lives together. I tried so hard to forget that I almost forgot you, too. Our past often makes up a great deal of what becomes of the future, but we must take from it what we can to make our lives and this world a better place. The lessons we learn in life, even the very hard and hurtful ones, may prepare us for what is yet to come. The past plays a great deal in who or what we may become, but it does not have to rule our lives if we learn from it. Do you understand what I'm trying to say?"*

*Tressa smiles, warming his heart. Although there are tears welling in their eyes, they are happy. "Then, I will name him Dancer," she says. "That's your name, Boy—Dancer. I'll never forget." She hugs the puppy.*

*Killian hugs his child, maybe realizing for the first time just how intelligent and complex Tressa has grown to be. Her strength and will reminds him of Miranda.*

"Daddy, wake up. The bad men are coming. Please. Oh, please wake up. The bad men are coming back!"

Killian jerks. Rising from the depths of darkness is no small task. His battered body is being sapped of its remaining strength. His tortured mind has been cascading into something that is frightfully close to an acceptance of fate.

Prophet forces his swollen eyelids to open, focusing to listen for any sign of their captors. Convinced that they are alone, he looks to the cage where his sick child and lover are lying motionless. Killian's eyes burn with the recollection of Essie's defilement, and the cruel joke played on him.

His wrists are petrified wood, numb and tingling at the same time. His fingers are inflated. By holding his unconscious 200 pound frame in suspension for so long, the handcuffs have begun to cut into the meat. His entire body, every cell, begs to die.

Killian's loaded right leg is extremely painful. The knee has swollen from the vicious blow with the nightstick. Nevertheless, this is the very leg he will have to lift above his head to get to the sneaker. He grips the iron bar, painfully.

With great effort, he attempts to raise the howling limb above his head, but it will not go. Fire sears through his nerve endings to push him to the very brink of fainting. A furious wave of nausea sweeps over him, churning the burning acids to his throat.

Tressa is growing sicker by the minute, laboring to complete every breath. There is a horrible rattle in her chest each time she coughs. The child has been Killian's strength in a time of great need. Now he has to summon his own reserves to save her from the cruelties of the world.

With his leg burning, Killian focuses on a nail on the opposing wall. He raises his left leg over the iron rod above him. Then, with all of his being, he forces his right knee to obey the command to bend. Throughout this excruciating effort, he remains focused on the nail's head, driving it further into the wood with his mind. It sparks with each metal-to-metal blow until it is done.

He wills his throbbing fingers to work on the shoelace, supporting most of his weight with the left leg. Removing the shoe seems quite impossible. Once the sneaker is free of the bloody sock, it slips and nearly falls.

As it swings from the handcuffs by the lace, threatening, Killian's racing heart thuds in his chest. He is afraid to breathe, whispering to God, "Please."

He closes his eyes, remaining motionless as it comes to a halt. After a moment of frantic thought, Killian captures the free lace with his teeth. He uses his nose and chin to push the sneaker upward until he can grab it.

He's just laid claim to the derringer inside when he hears a car approaching. Sweat begins to sting his eyes again.

What Killian is about to attempt will probably hurt, if not kill him, but he has to hurry. By positioning the derringer on top of the iron bar, he prepares to fire at the chain-link of the cuffs. He holds his breath, turning his face to focus on the nail that became his pinpoint of light at a long tunnel's end.

When Killian's clumsy finger presses the trigger, the gun fires, shredding his hands and legs with shrapnel. Faster than the speed of light, red-hot needles ravaged his flesh. The derringer flies from his grasp, and a scream erupts from his blistered lips.

Below him, the shiny metal of the gun glints atop an old bale of hay. As Killian's hands bleed fire, his heart sinks because he is still bound. He jerks and snatches at the cuffs, growling like a trapped animal. Outside, the sound of the vehicle fades, as if the car is passing by.

Killian's weight finally prevails upon him to drop his throbbing legs. He weeps, knowing abject failure. But just then, a grating metallic squelch comes from above as the link breaks, sending him crashing to the floor. He is sprawled there in a cloud of dust, amidst scattered hay, stunned from the painful shock of a sudden stop.

The sound of the approaching car resumes, much closer now, ripping Killian Prophet from his painful malaise. When the car stops, a door opens and slams shut. Officer Baker is coming. The writer hears heavy footsteps crunching in the snow. He has to move.

Baker opens one of the large doors just enough to slip into the cold barn. He's astonished to see that Killian is gone. The hairs on his neck prickle. He reaches for his weapon, wheeling at the sound of shuffling feet. The same baseball bat that he used to disable Killian Prophet crashes into the bridge of his nose.

The big bull goes down hard, but he is not out. Killian uses the bat to help him close the gap before Baker recovers from the blow.

Prophet's eyes are wild, furious orbs when he raises the bat overhead. He brings it down repeatedly, feeling shock waves from his bloody hands to his wounded knee. He hammers the cop's skull until his blood paints the immediate surroundings a violent rouge.

With his chest heaving, Killian Prophet looks down at his kill, feeling an evil surge of satisfaction. He drops the bloody bat and limps toward the cage, taking the key from a wooden peg on the wall.

Killian opens the cage, struggling to bend down. He pulls Tressa from the musty, rank bed of hay.

She is soaked and trembling from exposure. He not only hears the horrible rattle emanating from deep within her chest, he feels it. Killian holds his daughter close to his bosom and sobs. "Please be all right, Baby. Don't give up, Tressa. Please don't give up."

The child whispers, "Daddy, is that really you in there?"

Killian kisses her cheek, feeling a sense of relief, even though her eyes remain shut. "Yes, Sweetheart, I'm here. I love you so much."

Tressa coughs. "They're coming for us, Daddy. The bad men . . ." She slips away.

Killian places an index finger to Essie's throat and determines that she is also in crisis, when another door slams shut.

Sheriff Barnes has become impatient. Officer Baker was only supposed to check on the prisoners because they are having an early-morning meeting with his father to discuss the new gathering place for the Ku Klux Klan. Barnes regrets telling Baker about having his way with the woman, because his officer might have gotten ideas of his own.

Killian's heart hammers in his chest. He looks frantically at Baker's body, which rests on top of his weapon. The derringer has another bullet in the second chamber, but it is too far away. He has to do something quickly.

The door slips open on creaking hinges. "Damn it, Baker, I just said to check!"

Baker is lying in a pool of blood with his skull caved in. Sheriff Barnes looks up to see that his worst nightmare has escaped.

Barnes's mistake is in rounding the corner before he has completely drawn his weapon. A part of him screams at his abandonment of protocol, but a bigger part of him is certain that the writer has had sufficient time to take his people out the back way.

When unexpectedly faced with the enraged stare of a battered parent, Sheriff Barnes hesitates just long enough for Killian Prophet to drive the key to the cage into his right eye.

The sheriff sees a white flash, then screams in agony as his finger convulses on the trigger to send three shots into the wooden floor. The fourth shot penetrates his boot, taking a chunk out of his right foot.

Killian seizes the moment, wrestling the weapon from the sheriff's hand while in the grip of bipolar agony. With his left eye collapsed and a bullet hole in his right foot, Barnes cannot have anticipated a crunching blow with his own weapon. The heavy .45 slams into his jaw to send him crashing to the floor.

Something shifts in Killian's injured knee, seizing his entire body for a second. The pain is enormous, so he bends at the waist to ride it out on one leg.

With his swollen, trembling hands, Killian takes great pleasure in handcuffing the sheriff. Now he collects the sheriff's gun and drags Baker's Glock from beneath his wide bulk. After taking their keys to the cuffs, he checks to be sure that there is no one else.

He carries Tressa, one limping step at a time, to the squad car. Essie Dantzler will be much harder to deal with.

Upon his return, Killian takes the time to pull up Essie's jeans. Her legs are cold, and goose bumps seems to have set in for the duration. She moans his name when he cups her face to kiss her tenderly.

"Essie? Essie, can you hear me? I'm here for you, Sweetheart. I'm so sorry that I got you into this mess. I will find a way to make it up to you, somehow. Baby, we have to go now. Do you understand?"

He is delighted by her smile. Her eyes remain closed when she reaches out to caress his bristly cheek with drowsy affection.

"It hurts, Killy," she whimpers. "My head hurts so bad."

He sweeps the hair away from her bruised forehead. "I know," he says, "but I need you to try. Do you think you can do that for me?"

"I can't, Killy," Essie whispers. "You go. Take Tressa and go. She's so sick."

Killian bites his lower lip, shedding tears for her. He says, "I can't leave you, Essie. Try to get up, now. Come on."

She struggles to rise. When she finally opens her eyes, she thinks it best to keep them closed. Although dizzy, Essie forces her cramped body to rise with Killian's help.

Together, they take one step at a time. Once Essie and Tressa are situated in the front seat, Killian returns to the dilapidated barn.

Sheriff Barnes is beginning to come around.

A glint of metal catches Killian's attention, prompting him to retrieve the derringer. He looks at his sneaker and considers trying to put it on. When he picks it up, he removes the extra shells and tosses the shoe behind the musty bail of hay. If anything happens to him, the sneaker may be used as physical evidence.

The wounded sheriff struggles to his feet, cursing Killian Prophet to hell. He deliberately bumps into Killian's ailing right leg and drives his shoulder into the writer's mid-section. The weapons fall from Killian's belt and clumsy hands as he goes down!

Sheriff Barnes closes the gap quickly. With brutal impunity, he rams his left boot into Killian's gut and injured leg, ignoring the pain of his own right foot. His eyes rage as he waits for the right blow to the author's head to knock him out.

As the writer tries to get up, Barnes repositions himself. This is it. He cocks his left foot back, trying to bring it forward with all the force he can summon.

Killian's right hand closes around something small and metallic. He raises the derringer, dousing the sheriff's fire with yet another surprise. With the sudden shift, a bone snaps in Barnes's right foot and he crumples to the floor.

"Oh, Jesus!" the sheriff cries, unable to even touch the area of pain.

A moment later, Barnes tries to kick at the weapon, but his focus is flawed and his aim errant.

"Heel or die, Dog!" demands Killian. "Without hesitation, I'll kill you a thousand times if you don't do as I say. I've got a million and one reasons already." Roscoe does as he's told.

As Killian escorts Roscoe Barnes to the squad car, the wounded Anthony Barnes comes barreling up the road. Killian shoves Sheriff Barnes into the back seat, slamming the door on his injured foot. Moving toward the driver's door, he fires at the approaching car. He hits the windshield three times, barely missing the driver.

Anthony Barnes, with his hand and leg cinched tight to stop the bleeding, swerves into a snow bank.

Roscoe's squad car had been left running the entire time. When Killian puts it in gear, a metallic screech from the lower dash tells him that the other cop is firing back. Sparks fly from the radio when a bullet crashes through the passenger's door only inches from Essie Dantzler's head.

Killian floors it. Muddy snow flies from the back tires as he speeds down the semicircular drive. Anthony Barnes gives chase.

Just as before, Anthony Barnes tries the PIT maneuver, but his wounded hand makes things more difficult as both cars race down the country road. Mud and slush are flung through the air as they dip into harsh potholes, digging grooves where none existed before.

Killian also struggles to control his vehicle, grasping the wheel as tightly as he can with his inflamed, disobedient fingers. His wounded hands are bleeding more than before because the once-restricted blood vessels are free again.

Tressa's head bounces on Essie's lap. She is clearly having a nightmare as the sound of grinding metal invades her feverish realm. This was how it happened before, when Essie was driving.

Anthony Barnes takes the hand mike from the hook, but he puts it back. He thinks about what he is about to do, and involving others in the chase could expose them all. But the pain and the blood loss are beginning to take its toll on the sheriff's brother. For a split-second, his vision blurs. When it clears, he can see Roscoe's emaciated face in the rear window.

"Come and get me, Tony!" Sheriff Barnes shouts. "Don't you let this piece of shit beat you!" As if Anthony hears his older brother, he rams the car in front again, rattling Killian's teeth.

Roscoe is knocked to the floor by the blow, and his wounded eye and jaw scream when he falls face-first. Nevertheless, he struggles to right himself, refusing to let the agony stop him from taunting Killian Prophet with his profane declarations.

"You ain't gonna make it, Boy. I swear by God, we're gonna fry your black ass!"

"Shut up!"

Wham! Killian grits his teeth as his eyes flicker.

CHAPTER 18

# The Chase

*A*gent Davis runs into the room where Lee and Siegle are preparing to leave. "What is it?" Agent Siegle asks.

"There's an important call coming through. Agent Lee's line is busy and your phone must be dead. The call refers to this case." Siegle snatches the Blackberry.

"Agent Siegle speaking. Hello, is anyone there?"

"One moment, Agent Siegle—I'm putting you through right now. Also, new data pertaining to your recent database inquiries for the Prophet kidnapping is being downloaded. Is your unit prepared to receive?"

"Go!"

"Please continue to hold the line. Here is your call, Agent Siegle." When the switchboard connection is transferred, another voice comes across the line. The voice is a bit distorted so she presses the phone against her ear as firmly as she can.

"My name is Raymond Lampoon. I'm the owner of a private detective agency in Conway, South Carolina. I'm sending you my files on Killian Prophet."

With pensive urgency, Agent Siegle asks, "What's your connection to this case, Mr. Lampoon?"

"I'm afraid that I was the one who set him up, but I didn't know what they were planning to do. I was paid to conduct surveillance on Mr. Prophet and several others by men who I now know to be rogue cops of the Conway County Police Department."

"I need a name, Mr. Lampoon. Convince me with one name."

"Barnes."

"Sheriff Roscoe Barnes?"

"You know?" Lampoon asked, glad that he made this call. "Just how the hell do you know that?"

As the information comes through, Siegle says, "Never mind that. What happened, Mr. Lampoon? Where are you right now?"

Lampoon coughs up blood. Agent Siegle hears Lampoon say, "Just keep me alive, Doc." He coughs before going on to say, "My first surveillance contract was initiated and agreed upon under false pretenses. They told me that Prophet was a drug kingpin, using his writer's status as a cover. They told me that Prophet was hauling shipments of drugs through Conway by the waterway, so I traced his potential routes. They used the information to plot their entrance and exit routes to the Prophet home in Wilmington. They knew that my sister died of an overdose, so they used me to get what they needed. Then they forced me to do it . . . again."

Dr. Drescher applies pressure to Lampoon's wound on the kitchen table. His wife rushes in with clean towels.

"Are you injured, Mr. Lampoon?" she asks.

"The chopper's almost here," Agent Lee says urgently. "Let's move!"

Siegle saves all the data, then snatches the computer from the desk and heads for the back door.

"The sheriff's brother was sent to murder me when they found out that I kept duplicate files," Lampoon goes on. "That bastard tried to take me out right in my office."

"Anthony Barnes?"

"Yeah. They have Killian Prophet and his kid somewhere in Conway. I can't say where exactly, but I know they're here. You better hurry." He gasps and swears.

Siegle hears Dr. Drescher say, "You're going to die if . . ." Lampoon gasps again. The phone crashes to the floor, where it apparently remains. Siegle asks for an immediate trace because they have to protect Mr. Lampoon as a material witness, if he survives.

As the chopper lands on the beach behind Killian's home, Agent Lee shouts, "We're going hot, People. Get those ground units moving!"

They run to the beach and get into the chopper. Siegle immediately opens the Lampoon file. "Look at this," she says.

Agent Lee looks at the photograph of Killian and Miranda Prophet on the balcony of their Wilmington Beach home. The happy couple is engaged in an intimate moment. The time index was logged on the night before the first assault on the family.

"He's legit."

Killian's parents watch FBI agents pour out of both doors. They'd convinced Annabelle Dantzler, who'd left the hospital to return to her daughter's house to stay with them. In this twisted nightmare, the grieving woman now stands to lose the second of two children.

The poor woman is coming undone right before their eyes. She has taken to speaking to her dead husband, asking his forgiveness for having failed their children. She has aged so much.

Someone assigned to the family, explains recent developments, giving them a strand of hope.

Although Margo Firestone is confined to the Prophet estate under Agent Lee's authority, she does not contact her lawyer because guilt dictates that she swallow any bitter pill they force upon her. She joins the three parents in prayer, sharing tears that run like newborn rivers.

Anthony Barnes takes the left fork, which goes around a small pond. Both forks do, but the one Killian has chosen is the longer of the two because of its many curves.

Killian is relieved but remains cautious. He is moving swiftly, forcing the bruised Ford to blast through slushy potholes and patches of icy snowdrifts.

Essie whimpers, "He's up there . . . waiting."

"What?" asks Killian.

Barnes, knowing what his brother is planning, decides that he has to distract Killian. Essie's warning prompts him to say, "I fucked all her brains out. She's fucking delirious!" He laughs to taunt the driver.

"Shut up!" Killian growls with a glance in the mirror at his prisoner.

"He's up there." Essie tries to point a finger, but her hands feel so weak, so distant.

Barnes shouts, "She said that I'm up there on her top ten best list!"

Killian snatches a gun from the seat and aims it over his right shoulder at Roscoe's face. He says, "I swear to fucking God, I'll shoot you if you don't clam up!"

"He's up there, Killy!"

When Killian's eyes return to the road, he notices a pile of hay in a ditch to the right that seems out of place. Then he sees the bumper and back tires of Essie's wagon. Adjacent to it is a side road that intersects just ahead.

"He's up there!" Essie warns again.

Killian slams the brake pedal to the floor, causing the squad car to bow into a mud puddle.

Anthony Barnes has timed it perfectly, but he did not anticipate Killian's sudden stop. His squad car shoots across the road and passes inches before Killian's bumper to plow into the pile of hay that barely conceals Essie's overturned station wagon. Just as his car careens into the air, it obliterates the naked rear wheel of the Volvo and explodes. Essie's overturned wreck is forced upright by the violent collision.

Sheriff Barnes screams as his brother's squad car bursts into flames. It flips twice in midair before crashing to the ground upside-down

"Tony!" Barnes cries. Now he looks at Killian with purified hatred. "You're a dead man. You're fucking history!"

Killian floors it again, paying his prisoner's threats no heed. Moments after the explosion, Killian is just about to turn onto Parget Road when Anthonys' voice crackles over the airway. He is lying on the ground with his legs pinned inside the burning car. He can move his arms, but his back is broken. He has yet to realize that his legs are on fire.

"Officer down. This is car twenty-one, Officer Barnes." He coughs and gurgles. "I've been shot by a black male in his late thirties. Be advised that the suspect has taken Sheriff Barnes hostage and hijacked his squad car. He has also taken two other hostages—a woman and child. I think they're already dead. The suspect is heading east on Parget Road toward Highway 378. He is armed and dangerous. Please send help on Morgan Bridge Road. I repeat—officer down!"

As the fire reaches the parts of his body that he can feel, there is a horrifying scream. Squelch bursts across the frequency, then there is silence.

Killian takes the microphone from its hook and shouts, "That's a lie! My name is Killian Prophet, of Myrtle Beach. Barnes and his brother kidnapped my daughter. They tried to murder us. Please inform FBI Agents Lee and Siegle. Is anyone listening? I will not harm Sheriff Barnes unless I'm further attacked!"

When he lets go of the mike's key, it falls off. He looks at the neat bullet hole that bored through the mike and the dash. The radio is useless. Meanwhile, after getting Anthony Barnes's call, the dispatcher switches to another frequency.

"Shit! They can't hear me," Prophet says, and tosses the useless mike on the floor.

Sheriff Barnes glares at Killian. He's straining against the cuffs that only bite deeper into his flesh, indifferent to his race.

"That's right, they can't hear you. Even if they did, it wouldn't help because my men will splatter your brains all over that front seat as soon as they see your black ass. You're going to die, Motherfucker!" His collapsed eye sends a brilliant message of pain, causing him to grimace. Tiny spikes are driven into his retina, causing him to wail.

The highway lies ahead. Killian veers toward the ramp and pushes the engine to its limits. Light sleet begins to tap against the windshield. The weather is turning nasty.

Killian looks at his injured lover, whose eyes are shut. Her skin is pallid. Blood has resumed trickling down her forehead. Then he looks down at his child. Surprisingly, Tressa's eyes open for a few seconds. She is burning up, and her breath is coming in short puffs as her lungs work to feed her air. His eyes water when he notices that she has urinated on herself. As he has often written, a loss of bladder control is often a precursor to death.

Killian seeks out the sheriff's face in the mirror. His emotions are riding a razor-edged bullet, passing through fear and parental concern to utter contempt. His eyes now grow black, touching the one of his enemy in the rearview mirror. For a nanosecond, Killian sees the sheriff's awesome fear, before the man bolsters himself to resume the verbal abuse.

Roscoe's abuse, however, does not last for very long. His swollen jaw aches with each vile syllable and four-letter word that spews from his busted lips. His punctured eye is crying to see again. His busted foot throbs in a boot saturated with blood. The handcuffs are relentless reminders of his helplessness.

Barnes looks back, hoping to see signs of pursuit, but there are none. He knows that the radio is silent because the dispatcher is coordinating on another channel so Killian will not overhear their tactical plans. He is thinking he has to sit tight when they suddenly hear a chopper overhead.

## CHAPTER 19

# Damnation and Rain

Judge Barnes limps about the room, snatching his wallet and checkbook from the dresser. The old-timer is breathing hard as he tosses things into a bag. He instinctively looks over his shoulder before dialing the combination of the safe, removing all of its contents.

When his hairy earlobes tweak, he freezes for an instant and turns his head to listen to the eastern sky.

"Damnation and rain!" he spouts before rushing from the room. His bag hits the railing as he approaches the stairs, and to his displeasure, it falls from his grasp and scatters its contents on the way down.

"Damnation and *fucking* rain!" Judge Barnes shouts, again. He stumbles down the stairs to retrieve his papers and cash, but the clothes are left where they fell.

When he ambles out of his front door, his neat, orderly world goes crazy! The wind suddenly gusts and howls at him, as if in a demonic rage. As his eyes seek the descending chopper, his ears clearly discern the clatter of shotgun shells being racked.

A black police officer, for whom Judge Barnes holds no particular affection, orders him to drop the bag and put his hands in the air. He is ordered to his knees.

Judge Barnes takes a good look around as the chopper touches down, knowing that he is stuck without an out. As he bends those arthritic knees to comply, he considers the gun that spilled from the bag, quickly deciding that he would rather die than waste away in a filthy jail cell meant for common criminals.

When the judge reaches for it, the screen door is kicked open from behind. A stealthy state trooper places the barrel of the shotgun to the back of the old man's head. With no respect for age, the trooper places a boot in the judge's back and forces him to his stomach. With the weapon now out of reach, Judge Barnes sighs hard.

"It won't be that easy for you, Judge Barnes!" the trooper says.

The FBI agents, those who accompanied Lee and Siegle in the chopper, rush toward the house and direct the state troopers to search the grounds. It is snowing, but the pilot is ordered by Agent Lee to keep the rotor churning.

A moment later, Agent Siegle taps the keys of her computer with rabid urgency. Her instincts are telling her that this particular search will yield nothing.

A car races from the boathouse and slides to a halt. The driver shouts, "The boathouse is clear, but I believe we found blood evidence between the floorboards."

Another says, "The main house is empty, but I did find this." He holds up a copy of *Dark Eclipse*. Passages are highlighted throughout. A few pages are ripped out.

Angela says to Agent Lee, "Look here."

"What have you got?" Lee asks, hoping for something, because he knows that Judge Barnes will volunteer nothing. His phone rings. After hanging it up, he says, "The sheriff's property is clean. So is the brother's."

"Apparently, part of the divorce settlement was a 500-acre farm just north of here. Judge Barnes's ex-wife must have wanted nothing to do with this place, so she sold the property back to him to sever all ties. I found this through the property transfer of deeds and titles. That's got to be where they are."

The pilot shouts, "Sir, the weather is getting worse. I wouldn't advise that we take off at the moment."

Lee glares at the pilot before saying, "You're going to earn your pay today, is that clear? These people are in danger and we have to find them!"

Someone yells from the doorway of Barnes's home, "You'd better see this!"

Lee and Siegle run into the house, where Judge Barnes has neglected to turn off the television. Trooper Richmond joins them inside, once he has personally clamped Judge Barnes in irons and read him his rights.

A news chopper is shadowing a squad car, reporting dramatic events from above.

The excited reporter says, "The police are in hot pursuit as we speak. Vehicles are now traveling at dangerously high speeds for such bad road conditions. I can now see the police officer in the back seat of his hijacked squad car. From the position of his arms, he seems to be tightly bound." He gasps. "He appears to be badly wounded too. The driver appears to be a black male, but we are unable to get a clear picture of his face. There also appears to be someone, other than the driver, in the front seat of the squad car. The other fugitive is lying down on the seat, possibly to avoid the cameras. As you can see, the weather is becoming extremely hazardous out here, but we will stay with it as long as possible."

"That could be him," Agent Lee says. "Tressa's grandfather said he had a weapon. Prophet may have escaped! Somebody, grab a map."

Officer Richmond says, "No need for that. We monitored a call for assistance by Officer Anthony Barnes, the judge's younger son. His car crashed while in pursuit of the squad car. He also claimed that a black suspect shot him. We were moving to intercept when ordered to redirect. If we'd had more info at the time, this could have been avoided. Barnes crashed on Morgan Bridge Road, which would take him directly to Highway 378. Those are Roscoe's men after him right now."

"We've got to reach them before the local police exact retribution," Agent Lee says.

"You got it," Officer Richmond agrees.

Agent Siegle contacts the watch commander, ordering him to end the pursuit before his men do something stupid. The watch commander, however, is one of those who are supposed to attend Prophet's execution. He agrees to call the men off, but does not intend to actually do so.

They run from the house. Agent Lee splits his team in two, sending men north to check out the property on Morgan Bridge Road while he pursues the runaway cop car.

With a slight shiver, he orders, "Get this bird in the air!"

Killian is sweating. That could be Roscoe's men back there, and he's certain of what they will do if they're under the impression that he's an armed cop killer. Stopping is not an option. Tressa's eyes fly open. Her cold hand clutches her father's bloodstained shirt. She is silent, but calm.

"Tressa? Are you okay? Can you hear me?"

The child nods. She forces her sore, weakened body to rise from Essie's lap to embrace her father. He is relieved to see that she is fighting the rattling cough that's dragging her down.

"We're going to be okay, Baby," he says as he kisses her hand. "I promise. Stay down now."

The child shivers and clutches her father's midriff. Now her eyes flicker, which makes his heart seize. From the darkness that threatens yet again to envelope her, Tressa whispers, "Daddy, I'm afraid. God is coming for somebody. He's coming."

Killian checks her pulse, which has become chaotic. Her moment of consciousness gives hope, but those ominous words bring tears to his eyes.

"This is Edward Taper for News WTCW Skycam. We can see that a roadblock has been set up just beyond the Highway 501 overpass. A semi is ahead of the fleeing police cruiser. Wait, something's happening! The pursuing officers are attempting to overtake the fugitive on either side. Oh my! They're pointing shotguns at the driver." The reporter pauses, then resumes. "Apparently the driver of the semi has just seen the roadblock ahead. His trailer is now sliding sideways as he approaches the 501 overpass. Obviously, the roadblock has been poorly placed just on the other side of the overpass. He may have been looking in his rearview mirror at the pursuing squad cars."

With his face pressed against the glass, Roscoe Barnes shouts, "Shoot him! Shoot him, now, God damn it!"

Killian hits the brakes, holding the wheel straight with one hand and his daughter with the other.

They fire! The windshield is obliterated before Killian's eyes, as are the front driver and passenger windows.

As the police cars slide toward the fishtailing semi, Killian skids to the right, plummeting over the embankment. As the car plows toward Highway 501, the world turns black, gray, and white from muddy snow.

With the cold wind and slush blurring his vision, Killian regains control on the highway to Myrtle Beach. He tries to keep his child and lover warm by maxing out the heater.

"You fucking idiots," Roscoe curses from the back seat as he watches the two squad cars hurtle toward the semi. An explosion behind them is a deadly consequence of the ill-placed blockade.

High above, the news chopper's windshield wipers worked harder to clear the Plexiglas of sleet.

"We just witnessed a tragic event. Both the pursuing police cars have crashed into the swerving semi! There was a massive explosion, but the fugitive miraculously escaped by veering his car over the embankment. He's now headed toward the Savannah Highway bypass at breakneck speed. This is simply unbelievable!"

In the FBI chopper, Agent Siegle shouts, "There they are!"

"He's headed for another roadblock. This time there's a canal to the right and left. He can't possibly escape!" the pilot warns.

"Why haven't they removed the roadblocks?" the pilot wonders. "They're either . . ."

"Either hungry for blood, or they're in on the whole thing!" Agent Siegle finishes.

"It must go deep around here. Either Killian Prophet is just another cop killer in their eyes, or someone is privy to the planned abduction of Tressa Prophet to lure her father into their hands," Agent Lee suggests.

"We'd better overtake them. Hurry!" Agent Siegle says.

Four cars are blocking the icy road ahead of Killian Prophet. Two more are fast approaching from the rear. Snipers are readying their scopes to take aim at the driver of the hijacked police car, relaying every move to the nervous watch commander who refuses to call them off.

The snow is beginning to come down hard. Killian sees them in the distance, realizing that he only has one choice, which is to plow through. He pushes the gas pedal to the floor about 300 yards away.

In the chopper, Agent Siegle realizes what Killian is about to do and shouts, "Shit! Don't do it, Prophet."

Agent Lee tells the pilot, "Try to raise him on the radio again!"

The snipers are taking aim.

Nearly consigned to his fate, Killian looks down at his flagging child and lover. "God is coming for someone," he whispers to himself as tears stream down his face. He looks once more into the good eye of Roscoe Barnes.

Barnes sees that he means to do it, so he gets down on the floor and braces himself for all hell to break loose.

Suddenly there's a horrible noise as the brakes lock up. The car shoots forward with increasing speed. Killian tries to control it, but the car hits a patch of ice. As they spin out of control toward the roadblock, Killian leans over to cover his child and to hold onto Essie as best he can.

Around and around they spin, the world a blur of blended colors—even with his eyes shut!

Now, the car jerks harshly, and silence fills the dizzy world as Killian clutches Tressa. When he realizes that they have finally stopped, he raises his head to look about in disbelief. The car now sits perfectly straight in the middle of two lanes, as if by design.

He ducks just before the sniper's bullet comes through the busted windshield to obliterate the rear window. Roscoe smiles with a certainty that Killian's head has exploded with the glass, but he will be disappointed.

Crouched low, Killian reaches for the derringer. Remembering that there is only one bullet in it, he reaches under the seat and finds Officer Baker's Glock. As he moves about in the front seat, Sheriff Barnes smiles, convinced that Killian is convulsing in death. He really wants to look over the seat, but he knows better. His men will be along to free him shortly.

Killian looks at his child, touching her damp hair before opening his door to slide out. "Stay down, Tressa. Please stay down."

When Roscoe hears Killian's voice, he begins to shout, "He's got a gun in here! This animal killed Officer Baker and now he says I'm next! Shoot him, damn it!"

Killian opens his door and backs out, crouching low. He quickly snatches open the rear door and drags Sheriff Barnes out, using him as a human shield.

Even with a gun pointed directly at his head, Barnes persists. "Take the fucking shot!"

Killian looks back as the pursuing cars now slide to a stop. He wants to pull the trigger so badly that he can almost taste Roscoe's blood.

With his wild eyes blazing, he says, "I should send you straight to fucking hell. You are a murderous rapist of women and of children's worlds, and you don't deserve to live. You don't deserve to live!"

"Take the fucking shot. He killed Officer Baker and there's a dead kid in the car! Shoot him!"

"I have a clear shot," a sniper says.

With the snow distorting the world, Killian looks at Tressa. Her eyes meet with his in a moment of near-perfect clarity.

"You haven't got the balls to kill me," Barnes snaps. "They'll eat you alive in a second if you do. Go ahead and kill me, Motherfucker. I killed your bitch two years ago, and I'm going to kill you, too!"

Killian's eyes blaze, still locked in that gaze with his child. He says nothing more in response to Sheriff Barnes's taunts.

"Position two, take the shot. Take him out," someone whispers into a radio.

"Roger that on the snow kill," the sniper replies. He squints and caresses the trigger once with his gloved finger.

Killian suddenly tosses the gun and shoves Barnes to the ground.

The sniper rears up in surprise, but quickly returns his eye to the crosshairs as Killian raises his hands. The writer kneels, sliding his busted leg forward as his left knee hits the frigid pavement.

The sniper says, "Bye-bye."

Killian Prophet disappears from his view as a black chopper comes between them.

An amplified voice warns, "This is the FBI. The suspect is not to be harmed because he may be innocent of all charges. Stand down and holster your weapons. I repeat, stand down and holster your weapons. I'm ordering you to put down your weapons, or you will be shot!"

Tensions arise as loyalties are questioned. Who claims the authority to kill someone? Why does this man need to be killed so badly that the value of their own lives now comes into question?

Killian weeps as the snow thickens, churned by the rotor of the chopper. He had been willing to sacrifice his own life so that his child and lover might not come to harm by flying bullets.

Agents Lee and Siegle breathe sighs of relief, slide the doors open and step out. Looking at the runnels of ice that have formed all over the chopper, they are glad to be on solid ground.

"Shoot him!" Roscoe yells. "Shoot this motherfucker now!"

There is no response as an exhausted Killian Prophet collapses on the road.

In a moment that seems to move in slow motion, he watches as the FBI agents' eyes grow wide. They are running toward him, shouting, "No!"

Killian looks into the cab of the car, but Tressa is gone. He is struck by panic.

When he finally spots her on his left, he sees something shiny in her hand. "Tressa, no. Don't do it!" he cries as he tries to right himself.

Tressa stares into Roscoe's eye. She slowly raises the derringer, pointing it at his bloody face. Roscoe's eye bulges in disbelief.

Tressa Prophet now only hears her own heart beating. She looks back at her brave, wounded father, and then at Essie's unconscious form on the front seat. She returns her gaze to the sheriff. Her breath is coming in short, rapid puffs, but she manages to say, "This is for my family, Mister. God has come for you."

Just as Killian launches himself, she fires! He slides to an ungraceful stop at his daughter's feet. Standing before the sheriff's twitching body, Tressa lets the little gun fall from her grasp. When her eyes see what she has done, something very dark within, even at her tender age, finds satisfaction. Her eyes flutter and close. She faints into her father's arms, but the man who murdered her mother is dead.

". . . lest our children shall take up those arms to become killers themselves."

www.ingramcontent.com/pod-product-compliance
Lightning Source LLC
Chambersburg PA
CBHW030316180626
46810CB00003B/1108